The Book That Changed My Life is the outcome of a public participation project run by Scottish Book Trust in 2009. Scottish Book Trust invited people all over Scotland to write stories about the books that had made an impact on them. This book contains a selection of the most inspirational stories about books from members of the public and well known authors.

Scottish Book Trust is the leading agency for the promotion of literature, reading and writing in Scotland, developing innovative projects to encourage adults and children to read, write and be inspired by books. It is a non-profit organisation funded by Scottish Arts Council, sponsorship and other grants, based in the heart of Edinburgh's Literary Quarter on the Royal Mile.

For more information on Scottish Book Trust's projects go to www.scottishbooktrust.com

The Book That Changed My Life

Luath Press Limited

EDINBURGH

www.luath.co.uk

First Published 2010

in association with Scottish Book Trust

ISBN 978-1-906817-30-5

The paper used in this book is neutral sized and recyclable.
It is made from elemental chlorine free pulps sourced
from renewable forests.

Printed and bound by
CPI Bookmarque, Croydon CRO 4TD

Typeset in 10 point Sabon
by 3btype.com

Contents

Acknowledgements   9
Introduction   11

(stories by contributor surname A–Z)
Shams Abu-Tayeh's story about *My Life as a Man*   13
Hazel Allan's story about *Lamb*   14
Fay Bateson's story about *Alone Together*   16
Fanny Bernard's story about *Jane Eyre*   18
Alan Bissett's story about *Weaveworld*   20
Kenna Blackhall's story about *Stuart: A Life Backwards* 22
Sheena Blackhall's story about *Border Ballads*   23
Ali Bowden's story about *Danny the Champion of the World* 25
Caleigh Bradbury's story about *Black, White and Gold* 26
Gordon Brown's story about *The Fog*   28
Tom Bryan's story about *Walden; or, Life in the Woods* 29
Jennifer Bryce's story about *The End of Mr Y*   31
Myra Christie's story about *The Golden Treasury*   33
Mark Cousins' story about *A Portrait of the Artist as a
  Young Man*   35
Brian Cox's story about *The Dice Man*   36
Mark Coyne's story about *The Catcher in the Rye*   37
Kevin Crowe's story about *Dancing on the Edge*   38
Hunter David's story about *The Once and Future King* 39
Myra Dee's story about *Southeast Asia on a Shoestring* 41
Senga Dinnie's story about *The Unwanted Child*   42
John Gerard Fagan's story about *Shantaram*   44
Rob Fletcher's story about *1984*   46
Simon Fraser's story about *Superman:
  From the '30s to the '70s*   48
Janice Galloway's story about *Piano Course, Book A
  (The Red Book)*   49

Diana Sofia Gamio's story about *Tuesdays with Morrie*   51

Martin Gillespie's story about *It*   52

Camilla Gordon's story about *Noughts and Crosses*   53

Christina Gorrie's story about *Daffodils*   54

Jenni Green's story about *Swallows and Amazons*   55

Robbie Handy's story about *Portrait of a Young Man Drowning*   57

Caroline Henley's story about *The Boy with the Bronze Axe*   59

Grant Johnson's story about *The Easy Way to Stop Smoking*   60

A.L. Kennedy's story about *The Restaurant at the End of the Universe*   62

Jared Kropp-Thierry's story about *The Sopranos*   63

Kenny Logan's story about *Lassie Come-Home*   65

Kirsty Logan's story about *Horrible Histories*   66

Caroline MacAfee's story about *A Dictionary of the Older Scottish Tongue*   68

Ian Macfarlane's story about *The Mists of Avalon*   69

Ann MacLaren's story about *Heidi*   71

Drew MacLellan's story about *DK Dinosaur Encyclopaedia*   73

Alexander McCall Smith's story about *Collected Shorter Poems*   74

Andrew McCallum's story about *Linmill Stories*   76

Robin McCallum's story about *1984*   78

Martin McGale's story about *A Clockwork Orange*   79

Oisin McGann's story about *The Lord of the Rings*   80

Sara-Jane McGeachy's story about *Tiger-Pig at the Circus*   82

Pamela McLean's story about *Not the End of the World*   83

Elizabeth McNeill's story about *The Horse's Mouth*   85

Ishbel McVicar's story about *Liza of Lambeth*   87

Jacqueline Mercer's story about *You Can't Afford the Luxury of a Negative Thought*   89

Ewan Morrison's story about *Tropic of Cancer*   91

Margherita Muller's story about *The Shadow-Line: A Confession*   93

Donald S. Murray's story about *Kidnapped* 94

Ruan Peat's story about *The Count of Monte Cristo* 96

Elaine Pomeransky's story about *The Diary of Anne Frank* 97

Leon A.C. Qualls's story about *Swing Hammer Swing!* 98

Elaine Renton's story about *The Forest is My Kingdom* 100

Mark Rice's story about *The Hitchhiker's Guide
to the Galaxy* 102

Carolyn Roberts's story about *Longmans English Larousse* 104

Pauline Rodger's story about *Across the Barricades* 106

Michael Rosen's story about *Great Expectations* 108

Jane Rowlands's story about *Little Women* 109

Esther Phoebe Rutter's story about *Sunbathing in the Rain* 111

Jane Ryan's story about *Asterix in Switzerland* 112

Saïd Sayrafiezadeh's story about *Krapp's Last Tape* 114

Alex Shepherd's story about *War Picture Library* 116

Sara Sheridan's story about *Water Music* 117

J. David Simons's story about *Ulysses* 119

Cameron Sinclair's story about *101 Essential Golf Tips* 120

Andy Stanton's story about *The Wasp Factory* 121

Margherita Still's story about *Green Eggs and Ham* 122

Gael Stuart's story about *We Learned to Ski* 124

Marsali Taylor's story about *A Guid Cause* 125

Peter Urpeth's story about *Hunger* 127

Emma Walker's story about *Alice's Adventures
in Wonderland* 128

Heather Wallace's story about *Emma* 129

Rosie Wells's story about *Heidi* 130

Gillian Whale's story about *The Iron Man* 132

Michael Williams's story about *Siddhartha* 134

Eric Yeaman's story about *A School Chemistry for Today* 136

Sarah Zakeri's story about *Reading Lolita in Tehran* 137

Index of Books 139

Acknowledgements

Scottish Book Trust would like to thank the following people for their involvement and enthusiasm: Stephen Jardine, Ian Rankin, Lulu, John Michie, Craig Hill, Anthony Horowitz, the Readership Development Librarians of Scotland, the teachers and pupils of Bishopbriggs Academy, Carolyn Becket and Serena Field at BBC Radio Scotland, Sara Sheridan and Margherita Still and everyone who submitted their stories to the project.

Introduction

A BOOK IS AN inanimate object like no other. Books can inform and surprise, they can inspire and entertain, they can shock and console. A book can be friend, teacher, therapist, agitator and seducer. A book can bond with its readers and touch them in untold ways. Books can change lives.

'What are you reading right now? Have you read anything good recently? What is the best book you ever read? What was your favourite book as a child?'

This is the kind of dialogue which regularly takes place about books – the commonplace conversations which happen all over Scotland every day. Scottish Book Trust wanted to delve deeper into the profoundly personal relationships that people experience with books. We asked people to spill the beans on their literary love affairs – which book changed your life?

Whether a treasured childhood book which opened up the magical realms of imagination, a confidence-boosting self-help book that helped with a difficult time or a book that quite simply opened up a reader's love of literature – the spectrum of stories we received in reply ranged from the nostalgic and grateful, to the inspired and impassioned and all the way to the eureka moment of change and stunned realisation.

We have enjoyed reading these stories – as we hope you will – and have been inspired to read some of the books; not only might they be a great holiday read – they could change your life too.

Marc Lambert
Chief Executive of Scottish Book Trust

SHAMS ABU-TAYEH'S STORY

My Life as a Man

by Philip Roth

SYNOPSIS

A novel in two sections, partly autobiographical, about the trials of writing, marriage, disappointment and how fictions are constructed from life.

MY STORY

At first reading, I couldn't stand this book. But something about it intrigued me, so I went back for a second reading; as the book itself is written in what seems to be a random collection of chapters, this time I didn't start from the beginning.

The narrator writes in fits and starts, picks up the timelines and retells the story of his life and loves, over and over, differently each time. So, I took this on board and reread the book over and over again, starting each time at different chapters, jumping back and forth and, eventually, after many readings, starting from beginning to end again and seeing, finally, how it made sense. It clicked.

So, why did it change my life? How did a book of '70s New York narrated by a divorced and deeply bitter man about his confused life and relationships with women (a book sometimes reviewed as being misogynist) appeal, in fact deeply click, with a '90s teenage girl growing up in an Arabic country? Thinking on it, I believe it was the honest showing of the vulnerable insides we all carry, the bits that bleed and make us squelch – the realisation that other people out there, even apparently adult and sorted, can be feeling all this and share it – and more importantly, to make art out of it. For a growing youth with pretension to a future in writing too, it was heartening to see how there was a way to harness life's blows and make them into a book. That, though time can be confused, the confusion can be used as a tool; though hearts can break, those cracks can be literature; and that though sadness can permeate, a touch of humour can make it all a bit better.

My copy of that book, with its ripped and taped black paper cover, is one of those items that still makes me sigh in sadness, remembering leaving youth and my childhood country, moving to the very country Roth lived in.

HAZEL ALLAN'S STORY
Lamb
by Bernard MacLaverty

SYNOPSIS

This short novel tells the story of a young priest, Michael Lamb, who runs away from the Irish borstal that he works in, taking a deprived boy named Owen Kane with him. But, as his money dwindles, news of the kidnapping closes in on them and Lamb finds himself running out of ideas on how to save the boy's life, leading to a dark climax borne of both necessity and love.

MY STORY

I was 14 when I read *Lamb* for the first time as part of a school project. Bernard had lived next door to me when I was growing up so it made sense that my first adult novel should be by somebody I knew. I instantly became completely absorbed by it.

As a teenager and an aspiring writer *Lamb* was an inspiration to me. It taught me that literature had emotion, that it could make you cry buckets and that it could haunt the imagination for a long time after the final page had been read. This book was an awakening for me. Never before had a story evoked such strong emotion and in doing so it uncovered my own interest in writing about the big emotions such as love, grief and being an outsider. MacLaverty continues to be a most important influence in that respect.

This was the first book that I read that didn't have a happy ending. It was a startling introduction to the concept that justice does not always prevail, a sudden induction into the world of social realism. It was the first book I read that made me cry. MacLaverty's writing is never 'flowery' but is dark and honest. At 14, I was desperate to know about the truths of life however distressing and grim they might have been. I was ready to break free from my sheltered upbringing. And here I was being drawn into a story that actually made me feel like I was involved in the relationship with the man and boy. I began to understand the basic human need for affection and the sacrifices that are often made in the name of love. I remember feeling so desperately sorry for Owen, a boy who was not much older than I was at the time and yet our lives could not have been more different. A boy who I wanted to reach out and help; a boy who I would later come across in many forms during my career working with vulnerable and 'damaged' children. Owen Kane was the first character in literature that I really invested my feelings in. As a result, when the gut-wrenching climax came I was left so emotionally shattered that I felt that my life would never be the same again.

FAY BATESON'S STORY
Alone Together
by Sherrye Henry

SYNOPSIS

Virginia is a single, successful Wall Street analyst and a mother of two teenage children by a former marriage. She has a passionate but short-lived affair with Mike, a dynamic, self-willed New York businessman. In spite of opposing values on many things, can they learn to compromise and find a future together or does Virginia want to face the future alone?

MY STORY

Perhaps it was the personal resonance of the title which attracted me, reflecting, as it did, how my own life felt. After 20 years of increasing unhappiness I had reached a point in my marriage where reading about a relationship which demonstrated compromise and caring offered an escape from the reality of my situation. My personal life did not mirror the successful career which, though necessary for the family finances, no longer offered enough compensation for the battleground my marriage had become.

Alone Together explored and illustrated how Virginia and Mike (who had very different priorities), when faced with conflict, eventually learned to respect and accommodate each other and moved toward both space and togetherness. The significance of the story for me was not in the narrative. There was a reflective quality throughout the pages which made me realise that Virginia had achieved something I too sought. Somehow the author had managed to create an atmosphere so different from my own destructive relationship. It confirmed there was another way. Although it would include chaos and upheaval, I could change my life if I would only take the risk.

So I jumped! I said yes to a job in London and the distressing process of separation and dismantling joint lives began. The first six months were terrifying. The job was tough but manageable and in its own way exhilarating. Above all the sense of fear and tension was replaced by tentative optimism and hope.

Twenty-two years and a few continents later, and accompanied by a silver-haired rogue with an irreverent attitude to life and enough generosity and kindness in his heart to encompass the world, my big adventure and new life continue.

The novel is still on the shelf, dog-eared and yellowing, but it still represents the best £1.99 I ever spent.

FANNY BERNARD'S STORY

Jane Eyre

by Charlotte Brontë

SYNOPSIS

Jane Eyre is an orphan, dependent on the charity of an aunt who treats her cruelly. She is sent to boarding school aged ten. Eight years later, she leaves her position as a teacher to become a governess at Thornfield Hall, where she meets the enigmatic Mr Rochester.

MY STORY

I was 11, and in my first year of high school. A friend who shared my love of reading lent me *Wuthering Heights*, praising it highly. I read the book, but didn't like it much. The story didn't touch me and the characters all shared names, which confused me. But I was curious enough to look up other Brontë books on the shelves of my school library. There was an ancient, dog-eared, yellowed copy of *Jane Eyre*, by the sister of the author of *Wuthering Heights*. No blurb on the back cover, no note on the author. Just this portrait, in pencil, of a woman with soft brown hair, intense eyes, and the hint of a smile. I borrowed the book. It was the Christmas holidays. I started it one morning, lying on my bed, wondering if the first few chapters would be good enough to take me through to the end of this 600-page brick.

I couldn't put it down. I finished it in three days. Never had a book made me feel that way. Never had a narrator swept me away the way Jane did. Her voice, so warm, so clear, so evocative, so able to describe emotions, feelings, impressions. The suspense of the plot, full of highs and lows, the mystery, the atmosphere, the incredible revelations and dramatic events. The powerful presence of Mr Rochester, his irrepressible relationship to Jane... For me, at that age, who knew nothing of love, the force of this book, of this relationship, shaped my vision of life. The emotions that it revealed in me bowled me over, and are still a part of me, 15 years later.

Since that first time, I have felt the need to read *Jane Eyre* once a year, every year. For the first few years, I read the translated version (I am French). Then, later on, I tried the book in English, and was incredibly grateful that the French translation had been so faithful.

Every sentence was familiar, every description and simile was the same, even though it was in a different language. As I grew up, I saw different things in *Jane Eyre*, I understood some things better, I was even able to set a critical eye on this beloved book, which is, I think, what true love is: seeing the faults in something or someone, yet still loving them so much you couldn't do without them. Now, when I read this book, even though I know it by heart, I am still so moved, so affected by it, I can see so much of myself in it, and it has made me love literature so much, that I can truly and unhesitatingly say that this novel has changed my life.

ALAN BISSETT'S STORY
Weaveworld
by Clive Barker

SYNOPSIS

Weaveworld is an epic adventure of the imagination. It begins with a carpet in which a world of rapture and enchantment is hiding; a world which comes to life, alerting the dark forces and beginning a desperate battle to preserve the last vestiges of magic which humankind still has access to.

MY STORY

When I was 14, I started hanging about with a guy called Thomas Tobias (or 'Toby', as he was called, since everybody had a nickname), who is still my best mate to this day. We all used to gather around the stairs round the back of our mate Moonie's house, having a laugh. At the time I was reading stuff aimed at what you'd now call Young Adults, sprightly novels about teen crushes. Being a hopeless romantic, Terry Edge's *Fanfare for a Teenage Warrior in Love* was my favourite.

That was until Toby loaned me his copy of Clive Barker's *Weaveworld*.

It was a novel about (it seems almost ridiculous to say it now!) a carpet into which a world had been woven, but it was created with such care and detail that the whole daft premise of it fell away, felt fresh and utterly convincing. Barker had come to fantasy through the horror genre, his classic film *Hellraiser* and *Books of Blood* stories. Barker's take on that most misogynist of genres was particularly smart, politicised and subversive. And very, very gory. So *Weaveworld* was never going to be Terry Pratchett.

At 600 pages, it was by far the longest book I'd ever read, replete with enough wonderment, creatures and colour to capture the child in me, enough big ideas to stimulate the emerging adolescent, and enough darkness and narrative complexity to satisfy the future adult. I suddenly saw the world in a whole new way. My head seemed to expand at the speed of light. I was energised by the book, and immediately read everything of Barker's. Toby and I would sit up in his bedroom at night talking excitedly about our favourite characters, the coolest scenes. I still can't experience *Weaveworld* without the smell of Lynx Java coming back. Soon, we both admitted we wanted to be writers, and swapped stories which were basic Barker rip-offs. Toby told me he thought my stories had potential though and that I should keep writing them. We dreamed about what it would be like to go into a bookshop and pick up a book with either of our names on it. My surname began with 'B'. If I became a successful writer my books might go next to Clive's! That was my motivation.

Neither would I have gone to university without Barker. Finding *Weaveworld* invigorated my reading at just the age when young, working-class males begin to lose interest in books entirely. There was no going backwards then though. I moved quickly onto the writers Barker name-checked: Stephen King, Ray Bradbury, H.P. Lovecraft, M.R. James, E.F. Benson, Bram Stoker, J.R.R. Tolkien, Edgar Allan Poe. After Poe, anything became possible. In fifth year of school, I attempted *Moby Dick*. Eager to pursue this journey, and to avoid getting a job doing manual labour, I left Falkirk and went to study English at Stirling University. That's when the fun really took off. It's still taking off.

'Nothing ever begins,' as the last line of *Weaveworld* runs, 'And this story, having no beginning, will have no end.'

KENNA BLACKHALL'S STORY

Stuart: A Life Backwards

by Alexander Masters

SYNOPSIS

Stuart: A Life Backwards is the true story of a homeless man who strikes up an unlikely friendship with a young author who goes on to tell the story of his life, 'backwards'.

MY STORY

Some might base their review of a book on the complexity of the writing, while others marvel at the literary genius, the length of the words or perhaps a clever and intriguing story line. For me, a great book is one that helps you see the world through new eyes. *Stuart: A Life Backwards* moved me, more than I thought possible.

At parts it compelled me to shriek with laughter, and other times to turn inside out with sadness for the stolen childhood of a small boy. It introduced me to Stuart: a drug addict, an alcoholic, a convict, a thief, a homeless man, out of work and out of luck, who, incidentally, I grew to love and root for at every twist and turn in his helpless life.

It also introduced me to a different Stuart; a young boy, a helpless victim, a misunderstood child. A boy that was thrown into the sliding doors that so many people face, but came out on the wrong side. Heading down a path of no return which would ultimately end in his tragic suicide. The story behind the homeless man in the street; someone's son, someone's brother, someone's friend. The explanation that brings understanding.

Tears ran down my cheeks and a knot churned in my stomach when I reached the end and said my own goodbye to Stuart.

His true story stayed with me for a long time after I closed the book and I often recommend it to family and friends, hoping they can get from it what I did. Empathy for those less fortunate, sadness that some people suffer so much in life while others live blissfully unaware, and incredible gratitude for all that I have.

SHEENA BLACKHALL'S STORY

Border Ballads

by William Beattie (editor)

SYNOPSIS

A collection of Scottish ballads selected and edited by William Beattie and published in 1952.

MY STORY

Once upon a time I wrote an essay. I was 13. My English teacher returned it, unmarked. 'It's too good for you to have written. It's obviously been copied.'

I was incandescent with rage. This particular English teacher had a very harsh, raucous voice which grated on the ear like a rasp. I vowed I'd pay no attention to anything she tried to teach me thereafter. Then one day she opened a book of Scots ballads and proceeded to read 'The Twa Corbies' like an incantation.

Most pupils struggled to comprehend it. I had no such problem. Scots is my Mother Tongue. As the ballad progressed, the hair rose on my neck. I was aware that I was listening to something very ancient, very powerful, which was working on different levels to engage me. Both sets of my grandparents were farmers; I was accustomed to seeing crows disposing of dead lambs, rabbits, or other carrion. Crows are nature's recyclers; there is nothing odd about the fact that they cleanse the byways of roadkill.

The ballad, however, made me aware of my own mortality. In mediaeval times death was open and accepted, in our society it is feared and hidden. The effect of hearing 'The Twa Corbies' was like that of having a false mirror smashed. Perhaps things weren't as sanitary as people pretended they were. How did other cultures cope with death? I discovered that the Parsees of India and the Tibetan Buddhists opt for sky burial... bodies remain unburied for the birds of the air to feast on, thereby continuing life's cycle. I discovered that the Celtic goddesses, the Morrigan and the Norse god Odin, had crows as followers. The Warlock Laird, Alexander Skene of Skene, kept crows as his familiars.

Visually, the ballad is grimly powerful. Two crows divest the corpse of a young knight of his mortal trappings. His hair is utilised as nest material, his beautiful sightless eyes are harvested for food. Meanwhile, his faithless hawk, hound, and lady, have already forgotten him and go about their business unconcerned by his fate. 'The Twa Corbies' is a peerless lesson on impermanence, deeply etched into the Scottish psyche.

Nowadays, I take pupils in schools on a voyage into the ballad. I insist at the offset that they sit in silence and shut their eyes. I then invite them to walk with me in their imagination down the centuries, back to an ancient beech wood, late in autumn. Leaves crackle underfoot. Mist swirls. From below an old dyke, comes the sound of crows cawing and flapping around something that interests them... I invite the listener to step nearer. And then, to an old Breton tune, I begin to sing the ballad...

ALI BOWDEN'S STORY
Danny the Champion of the World
by Roald Dahl

SYNOPSIS

A children's novel about Danny, a boy who lives an idyllic life with his father in a caravan. Together they embark on daring adventures, poaching pheasants and attempting to outwit their nasty neighbour, Mr Victor Hazell.

MY STORY

One of the best things in the world is to be read to, and when I was young, my teacher at school read *Danny the Champion of the World* to my class. We were a bit of a rowdy bunch so to make sure we all sat still, at the end of each day we had to sit with our hands and our heads resting on our desks. I think the general weirdness of sitting with all my friends with our noses smushed up against our desk, our breath making our faces hot, and above us the voice of our teacher reading, made the story even more vivid in my mind. And it is a great story. And it was about me. My dad fixed cars, just like Danny's dad. There were pheasants next to where we lived, just like Danny. That I wasn't a boy didn't really matter, because I was Danny. I'm not that young any more, but back then, it was someone taking the time to read to me that made me want to read, to hear more great stories, to find really good books. I still love it when someone reads to me, it's my favourite thing.

CALEIGH BRADBURY'S STORY
Black, White and Gold
by Kelly Holmes

SYNOPSIS

The autobiography of Dame Kelly Holmes, who writes openly about her life and achievements. From her mixed-race background, to her army career, her famous double gold triumph in the 2004 Olympics, and her recent retirement from athletics, this book charts the human emotions behind her indomitable outward personality.

MY STORY

Dame Kelly Holmes is the perfect role model for kids of all ages; she is a two-time Olympic gold medallist and has won numerous titles. She now coaches kids all round the country. She is also the London 2012 Olympics Ambassador. To most, this would sound like she's superwoman; but she's had her ups and downs, her good and bad choices, her injuries and her everyday problems. Her autobiography reminds the reader that even though Kelly Holmes is a top athlete and a very charitable person, it wasn't an easy journey for her: 'Crossing that line changed my life. Only seven days earlier, I had been someone with a dream.'

This book hasn't changed my day-to-day existence but it could have a big effect on my future. Before I read this book, I wouldn't have even considered thinking about joining any aspect of the armed forces, but now that I've seen what they can do for you, it is definitely one of my options. Holmes entered the army as a truck driver and then went on to be a PTI (Personal Training Instructor). She was never an academic person, so this was a great path for her to go down as she loved teaching her talents and was very athletic: 'I felt free and I was thoroughly enjoying army life.'

When reading this book, I couldn't wait to find out what Kelly got up to next in the army. Before I read the book, I thought the army was all about war and fighting, but now I see why people want to join. The army offers loads of opportunities. Even if you're just doing one of the office jobs, you will be offered opportunities of a life time and almost definitely have fun while working there.

'But the army; that was something else. It was more rough and tough and go-in-there-and-do-it.'

Right now, I'm thinking of becoming a medical doctor officer. This means I can do at least five of the things I want to do in the future all at the same time: be a doctor, join the army, play sport, manage a team and try new things. Even if I don't go into the army, it has given me a much greater respect for all those who have joined the armed forces.

GORDON BROWN'S STORY
The Fog
by James Herbert

SYNOPSIS

A horror novel in which a peaceful village in Wiltshire is shattered by a disaster which strikes without reason or explanation, leaving behind a trail of misery and horror. A yawning, bottomless crack spreads through the earth, out of which creeps a fog that resembles no other. Whatever it is, it must be controlled.

MY STORY

I'm sitting on the edge of my Gran and Grandpa's creaking old brass double bed. It fills every inch of the room and it is where I will divvy up the Scottish Cup tickets for the North East of Scotland for the 1976 cup final between Rangers and Hearts – my Grandpa was connected to the Scottish Football Association. It's the late summer of 1975 and I'm three floors up on the corner of Cross Street and Mid Street in Fraserburgh and the smell of the fish gutting factory is heavy in the air. I'm 13 years old and I've just finished *Tom Swift and His Cosmotron Express*. Tom and his friend Bud Barclay have just seen off the evil VIPER and I'm clean out of books. I've read every Hardy Boy, Tom Swift and Famous Five book going and my Gran walks into the room. 'I'm going to the library. Do you want anything?' she asks. 'A book,' I mumble. I'm so a teenager. An hour later she returns and drops James Herbert's *The Fog* on the bed. I pick it up and read the first line – 'The village slowly began to shake off its slumber and comes to life.' Life changed. People lopping off other people's private parts – blood – violence – SEX. I was hooked and the fact I read it from cover to cover that afternoon and went out the next day to get James Herbert's first book – *The Rats* – told me that Tom and the Hardy Boys were history. Since that moment I can't remember a day that I haven't had at least one book on the go – more likely three or four. I was, and still am, a book junkie. It is all so prescient now as I've just had my first novel published and I can trace it all the way back to that day in Fraserburgh. Without my grandmother's efforts to please her eldest grandchild I reckon my life as a novelist would have been stillborn. Thanks Gran.

TOM BRYAN'S STORY

Walden; or, Life in the Woods

by Henry David Thoreau

SYNOPSIS

Walden is an autobiographical account of Thoreau's time (1845–1847) in a cabin on Walden Pond.

MY STORY

It was 1968; the Year of Revolution and I needed something to make sense of my personal life and of the political life around me. Paris. Prague. Chicago. Race riots. The war in Vietnam. I needed peace and some guidance and there it all was. 'When I wrote the following pages, or rather the bulk of them, I lived alone in the woods...'

A life of simplicity, individuality, the road less travelled by; an elusive but worthwhile goal, sometimes a hard place to be for a writer just trying to pay the bills. However, I also like practical solutions and Walden is a practical book, full of bean fields, broken axes, rain and snow. It also soars into Hindu and Greek mythology and philosophy. As I grew older and read Walden at least once a year, I realised the depth and level of the book and how much it had given me.

Civil Disobedience is often an appendage to Walden and nearly at odds with it, but the two books dovetail. One day the State will come knocking on your cabin door and demand its pound of flesh. In Thoreau's case he went to jail for refusing to pay a tax which supported the notion that runaway slaves were property and that to aid human freedom was in a sense harbouring stolen goods. Thoreau made it clear that conscience made some collaborations impossible. In that time Vietnam, in later times, poll taxes or conscription.

Like Thoreau, I later lived in a cabin catching my own fish, tending an old shotgun, writing, and learning how much I could do without. A helluva lot. Simplify.

Walden has a theme of dawn, resurrection, renewal. 'However mean your life is, meet it and live it; do not shun it and call it hard names.' I have read that book perhaps 50 times but it remains as fresh for me today as the pure ice of his Walden Pond. It is no longer a book; it is just part of who I am. It is my desert island book. If I had to be Robinson Crusoe, then *Walden* would be my Man Friday.

JENNIFER BRYCE'S STORY
The End of Mr Y
by Scarlett Thomas

SYNOPSIS

A literature student comes across an obscure volume in a second-hand bookshop and embarks on a bizarre journey through literature, physics, religion and reality.

MY STORY

It's strange to think that *The End of Mr Y* is a book I haven't even finished reading. Nevertheless this book is the one that has changed, no, is changing, my life; I can feel it happening.

The thing is that, unlike so many other books that I love, it doesn't make me feel. I'm a very emotional person, making me laugh or cry isn't hard, but this doesn't, it does something else. *The End of Mr Y* makes me think.

Imagine your brain as a kind of machine, all cogs and wheels and gears and a big red start-button marked THINK. Every time you read a book or obtain a new piece of information it adds another cog to the machine, and when you press the button it chugs into life and you start thinking. Unfortunately my machine doesn't work like that; it clanks and clunks along for a little while and then it grinds to a halt, and the bigger the machine gets the harder it is to get it going. And then I read *Mr Y*.

It was like someone had slipped in while I was sleeping and coated the whole thing in grease and filled it with oil. I went to class the other day and hit the THINK button without much hope that anything would happen, but it did. Out of nowhere this big hulking thing began to work, and it didn't just chug, it purred.

Suddenly everything I'd ever learned seemed to connect and flow and it all made sense. It started with a simple connection that began to spiral outwards until stuff that I'd had only a vague grasp of before was making much more sense because it was now connected to something else.

I've studied literature for over four years now and, I'll be honest, it's been a slog; I love it, but sometimes it's hard. And now everything has started working and it's joyful. It feels as though I'm finally getting towards that intellectual potential people are always telling me I have, but I haven't yet been able to fully access. And it's all because of a book, though not one I would have expected.

The more I read of *Mr Y* the more blanks begin to fill in and the better that big thought machine of mine works. And while I worry that, when I do finish it, the oil will dry out and machine will grind to a halt once more, at least I know that it does work, which is more than it did before.

The End of Mr Y has allowed me to think, and I could never ask for anything better.

MYRA CHRISTIE'S STORY
The Golden Treasury
by Francis Turner Palgrave

SYNOPSIS

Francis Turner Palgrave's *The Golden Treasury* is the best-known anthology of English poetry ever published. Its aim back in 1861 was to teach 'those indifferent to the Poets to love them, and those who love them to love them more.' There have been several updated editions since then which have included Spenser, Shakespeare, Wordsworth, Tennyson, Yeats, Eliot, Dylan Thomas, George Mackay Brown, Ted Hughes, Philip Larkin and Carol Ann Duffy.

MY STORY

My love of poetry started by listening as my mother read to me from *The Golden Treasury*. I was five years old. My memory is of sitting by her feet, in front of a roaring fire, and I sat silently engrossed.

It was on one of these evenings, when my mother picked up the orange, hardback book, that she began to read the poems of Robert Burns and I was transfixed. I wept over 'Mary Morrison', 'John Anderson, my Jo' and 'The Banks o' Doon'. My mother worked in the Dundee Jute Mills and we had just moved to a new housing scheme, so I was not familiar with the countryside, but I remember the language, the images and the sounds created by such poems as 'Sweet Afton' with the images of its 'green braes, the sounds of its 'murmuring stream', 'the blackbirds' and 'the green crested lapwings'. I wanted to smell the 'woodland' the 'sweet scented birk shades' and 'the primroses'. My mind still conjures up those senses.

I began to read the poems for myself, many of which I did not understand, but I loved the rhythms, the rhymes and the sounds the words made when I read them aloud. My mother bought me a small, tartan bound book, *The Best of Robert Burns* which I dated, 22 July 1957. I was ten years old. I marked the poems I learned by heart, or which were my favourites. At school, I learned more about poetry, reciting and acting out parts.

My mother died when I was 15 years old, but I believe I was given a priceless legacy in the love of poetry. I even read hymn books because of the verses. In our early courting, my husband gave me *A Book of Scottish Verse,* his first gift to me.

As an adult at university I read poetry, but my choices began to take a particular slant. My favourite poet is Thomas Hardy for his love of nature and the countryside. I discovered the wonderfully descriptive writing of John Clare, whose acute concern for man's damage to the countryside contributed to his being committed to an asylum.

I see changes being caused by man to the environment. The images of nature extolled to me in poetry are disappearing and I am trying to help slow down these changes. I believe that the type of poetry I enjoy has made me appreciate the wonders of nature and how we live alongside its creatures, each contributing and playing its part in the survival of the planet. Much of this I owe to my first encounter with poetry from *The Golden Treasury,* which I heard at my mother's knee and I believe this first book helped shape my life.

MARK COUSINS' STORY

A Portrait of the Artist as a Young Man

by James Joyce

SYNOPSIS

This autobiographical novel portrays the early years of Stephen Dedalus. Each of the novel's five sections is written in a third-person voice that reflects the age and emotional state of its protagonist, from the first childhood memories written in simple, childlike language to Stephen's final decision to leave Dublin for Paris to devote his life to art.

MY STORY

James Joyce's *A Portrait of the Artist as a Young Man* blew apart my waning Catholicism in Belfast in the 1970s. I read it like a lifestyle manual. It decoupled me from the whisky breath of my nation, and made me want to be an explorer. I haven't cracked its spine in more than two decades, but am sure that I'd have had a far slower start without it.

BRIAN COX'S STORY

The Dice Man

by Luke Rhinehart

SYNOPSIS

A novel about living your life by the roll of the dice, the philosophy
that changes the life of bored psychiatrist Luke Rhinehart — and
in some ways changes the world as well. Because once you hand
over your life to the dice, anything can happen. *The Dice Man* is
one of the cult bestsellers of our time.

MY STORY

One of the most influential books I have ever read was called *The
Dice Man* by Luke Rhinehart, the pen name of George Cockcroft.
Of course, there are certainly better books that scale the heights of
man's journey, but the appeal of *The Dice Man* is that it fixes at a
point in time, a point when the idea of risk in life was very exciting.
The idea is that your life can be lived by a roll of a dice when
usually in life so much of the time we try to structure what we do
and how we live it, as if we are in control. But the truth is, I think,
that we are never really in control. What Rhinehart does in this
novel is turn this idea on its head and sends you into an unknowing
and challenging destiny, all based on the shake of a dice. This book
has been republished many times over the years, and even at times
been banned. However, each new generation that discovers it, finds
I think, aspects to relate to and in a way this is what keeps the
novel timeless – it speaks to many generations. In my generation for
example, it was about dare and risk and a dispelling of the notion
of any kind of certainty. A very challenging, funny, revealing and
witty book.

MARK COYNE'S STORY
The Catcher in the Rye
by J.D. Salinger

SYNOPSIS

The classic coming-of-age tale of teenage cynicism, angst and rebellion, this novel charts two days in the life of Holden Caulfield as he rails against the system, adults and dumb people in general.

MY STORY

I thought *Catcher in the Rye* was the most boring book I'd ever come across. I had picked it up, aged 17, on the advice of my friends (we were all pretty angsty teenagers at the time); I was reliably informed with some amount of zeal that it would change my life, and I suppose they were right about that.

It was only with hindsight I realised this was a defining moment in my life. I had been a 'noncormist, just like my friends' for years, but the debate that followed was the first time that I felt my own mind and opinions differed more than most in my immediate vicinity. Ten years later and my sense of indignation has mellowed (although only slightly) at Holden Caulfield and his whining. But having thoroughly trashed this book, I would still recommend anyone who hasn't read it to do so, because it did for me what good literature the world over is supposed to do... It acted as a catalyst to independent thought.

KEVIN CROWE'S STORY

Dancing on the Edge

by Richard Holloway

SYNOPSIS

The former Episcopal Bishop of Edinburgh argues that gay people should be welcomed by all denominations, that gays have a lot to offer and that churches should apologise for their treatment of gays.

MY STORY

I grew up in the 1960s both Catholic and gay, and couldn't reconcile the two. I ended up denying both my sexuality and my religion. Some years after coming out, whilst managing an HIV/AIDS project, my admin worker – who was also training as a Methodist preacher – gave me a copy of *Dancing on the Edge*. Its effect on me was momentous. I had for some time become less antagonistic towards the Church, and after reading this book – in which Richard Holloway argues that gay people have a lot to offer all denominations – I attended Mass at a nearby Dominican priory.

The sermon was all about not judging people. After Mass, I saw a priest wearing a leather jacket and an AIDS ribbon, so I nervously approached him. It turned out he was the Catholic hospital chaplain and convenor of Quest, the Catholic gay organisation. He took me back into the Church. It felt like coming home.

That was about 15 years ago. My partner of 20 years has since joined me in the Catholic Church (moving from the Church of England). We are in a civil partnership, and we received lots of support from our local church – both priest and parishioners.

HUNTER DAVID'S STORY
The Once And Future King
by T.H. White

SYNOPSIS

A re-working of Mallory's *Morte d'Arthur*, written ostensibly for children but with adult wisdom – simply told with deceptive depth. The book remains true to Mallory in telling the story of Arthur and his knights but through the prism of the author's experience of the first half of the 20th century. Ultimately, the story is a tragedy as might triumphs over right but, even in defeat, the struggle is worthwhile.

MY STORY

I first read *The Once and Future King* in my early teens, at a time when boys read stories of fantasy and adventure. But I found a book that was more than just a ripping yarn. T.H. White is a romantic with an idealised vision of the Middle Ages, in reaction to the awful things he sees happening in the modern world. Nevertheless, like his characters, he tries to make sense of what is happening and is too honest to find simple answers or simple villains. It is not easy trying to live up to your ideals and the main characters all struggle – and fail – in various ways. Yet their struggle is all the more heroic because of their weaknesses. And sometimes struggle is all we have.

The life-changing part for me was the description of Lancelot – 'the ill-made knight' – who, despite public acclaim, suffers from bouts of depression and mental illness. Lancelot believes himself unlovable. He looks at his reflection and sees only his own ugliness. He struggles always to be good because he sees a blackness within himself and is afraid of the monster he thinks he will become if he ever lets go. I could identify with that and how many other children fear they are unlovable or feel guilty about the 'darkness' of their 'true' nature?

Through this book, I began to come to terms with myself. If I could sympathise with Lancelot, I needn't be so hard on myself. At the start, just knowing that others felt these things was a revelation and a comfort. Later, it gave me tolerance and understanding of others as I grew up and out of my own childhood and teenage angst.

But the book is so much more. It is a story well told and an old story retold. And it has all the rich detail and complexity of a finely woven tapestry. Arthur is the 'candle in the wind', trying to do the right thing against the odds and, if that is not an inspiration to generations of young and old idealists, it should be.

MYRA DEE'S STORY
Southeast Asia on a Shoestring
by Tony Wheeler

SYNOPSIS

A travel guide to Southeast Asia giving specific information for travellers on a budget, covering Thailand, Vietnam and Malaysia.

MY STORY

I had saved up for my trip to Thailand for a long year and a friend, who had been already, suggested that while I was there I might explore more of the area. The flights cost a lot but she said, once I was there, travelling to and fro in the area would be very cheap and easy. I was nervous about it; I'd always just gone on package trips to places like Greece and Spain. I didn't know what to expect and thought I would get lost or ripped off or put myself in danger.

My friend recommended this book and I excitedly read each section through in the weeks before my trip.

When I arrived in Bangkok I was feeling nervous and excited but also proud of myself, like I was an intrepid explorer facing a new land for the first time. I will never forget the butterflies in my stomach as I walked onto a Thai beach at sunset for the first time. One night in my first week there, someone stole a bag from under my table and I remember the panic as I searched through my remaining bag to make sure that my wallet, passport and this book were still there – I was so relieved when they were all safe and sound! I felt angry for a while but then realised that the worst had happened and I was still there, still enjoying myself and it wasn't the end of the world.

Southeast Asia on a Shoestring gave me the confidence to travel around and discover new places by myself. It gave me such a great feeling of independence. I felt as though there was nothing I wasn't capable of!

I still have my battered old copy sitting on the shelf to remind me of those great times on my trip of a lifetime.

SENGA DINNIE'S STORY
The Unwanted Child
by David Pollock

SYNOPSIS

This is an unpublished poem written by my father, in 1941.

MY STORY

I was a nine-year-old school girl when I first became aware of my father's poetry writings. This was revealed during one of the many lively debates which frequently occurred around the family dining table.

The dining table was the forum for chit-chat in our house at that time; the entire family gathered to eat their evening meal, affording each member opportunity to impart episodes of events in their day worthy of sharing. It could be a time of great merriment and joy, or on occasions, huffs and heated arguments.

One night, my brother Murray, 13-years-old and a secondary school pupil, informed the family of his contribution to the final day holiday class concert; a poem, by David Pollock, my father, entitled 'The Unwanted Child.'

My parents nearly choked on their meal with the mood turning quite tense and serious. I recall my mother anxiously asking where he had learned this poem and seeing my brother glance accusingly at my father, who in turn unashamedly, and in fact, rather proudly admitted to providing this script, but clearly defended his position: 'Never for a minute did I think he would present a performance of my work of art in front of his whole class!'

My brother was encouraged then and there to repeat his rendition and my heart filled with pride at the realisation that this poem was about me! I felt so important that day and any reference to being 'unwanted' didn't even register. The sombre mood at the tea table fired my celebrity status: me, the subject of a poem, written by my father then recited by my big brother in his school concert! My expressed excitement sent the whole table tittering with laughter. I've come to realise it was not the most flattering sentiment to read about oneself but my lasting memory on that occasion, with my entire family around the dining table, was having all their attention focused solely on me. For the first time experiencing the limelight and feeling fleetingly special was pivotal in my life. It shaped my attitude and has, I believe, equipped me in adulthood to see the humour in many situations, to laugh at myself but most importantly to remind me that there is generally a positive aspect to be found even from the bleakest beginnings!

'The Unwanted Child' by David Pollock

> Twas on a dull October morn
> The unwanted child was born;
> Unwanted, that is what I say –
> Her mother cursed the very day
>
> Although I said she was a lamb,
> Her mother didn't care a damn:
> Had you seen her at that early hour
> You'd think her just a lovely flower
>
> Friends came from near and far
> To gaze upon the new born star...
>
> Senga is her name,
> (In case you doubt) – that's Agnes turned round about!
> And I'll always say, you'll bless the day,
> When Senga comes your way.
>
> October, 1941

JOHN GERARD FAGAN'S STORY
Shantaram
by Gregory David Roberts

SYNOPSIS

Shantaram is a novel about the epic journey of an escaped Australian convict, who acquired a fake New Zealand passport and ended up in Bombay, India.

MY STORY

It was three days after my 23rd birthday when I heard the news. I was living in Australia: a trip of a lifetime was turning into a living nightmare.

I'd finished my degree and headed to Australia with Mikey, Bob, Tony and Phil: friends I'd known since primary school. We crammed into a tiny Sydney apartment and had a fantastic time. We later got jobs in Home-Hill, a town just outside the city of Townsville.

I'd worked 30 days in a row and left a few weeks earlier, heading down the coast with Bob and Mikey. Phil was short on cash and stayed.

After Brisbane, Mikey went to Melbourne while Bob and I headed to Byron Bay. Mikey phoned at five am He said Phil had been violently attacked in Home-Hill. He was in a coma. He didn't know any details and couldn't get to Townsville for three days. I got the first bus and stayed on it for 28 sleepless hours.

At the hospital I saw Phil in intensive care. His face was twice the normal size and part of his skull was missing. It was the most horrific sight I have ever witnessed.

I remember waiting for Phil's parents to arrive from Scotland. How do you tell your friend's mum that her 20-year-old son is dying; might even be dead? I can still hear his mum's scream. I was frozen, numb, staring at the floor. The doctors said he was still alive but effectively braindead.

Everything was crumbling around me. That night Tony gave me *Shantaram*, a novel by Gregory David Roberts. I remember looking at this 936-page book, with a red silhouette of Indian buildings over a blue background. It looked like some torturous new age, self-help book. *Shantaram* is a fictionalised autobiography.

Roberts escaped from an Australian prison, acquired a new identity and ended up in India. From the very first page I knew this book was something special.

Three days later Phil showed his first signs of life: he moved his right hand and his brain signals improved. We finally allowed ourselves some hope.

Phil 'died' another seven times in hospital. Bob, Mikey and Tony had left now, but at night I wasn't alone. I was hundreds of miles away on the run with Linbaba. I read how Linbaba dealt with the death of his closest friend. Each night that book took me far away and kept me there until I finally fell asleep.

Phil recovered enough to get a flight back home with his mum. The doctors said it was a miracle.

Shantaram helped me cope with the most difficult period of my life and made me want to be a writer.

ROB FLETCHER'S STORY

1984

by George Orwell

SYNOPSIS

Hidden away in the Record Department of the sprawling Ministry of Truth, Winston Smith skilfully rewrites the past to suit the needs of the Party. Yet he inwardly rebels against the totalitarian world he lives in, which demands absolute obedience and controls him through the all-seeing telescreens and the watchful eye of Big Brother, symbolic head of the Party. In his longing for truth and liberty, Smith begins a secret love affair with a fellow-worker Julia, but soon discovers the true price of freedom is betrayal.

MY STORY

As Robin and Margaret Fletcher eased their battered van into gear and began their journey back down a road pitted with cavernous potholes, they traded a look of grave concern. For they had just dropped the tall gaunt figure of Eric Blair off at a crumbling cottage on the edge of the world. A writer, apparently, Blair was determined to exist in this isolated outpost on the Island of Jura. But how, the Fletchers wondered, would this frail and cadaverous southern intellectual cope with the harsh reality of Hebridean life? The year was 1946 and their passenger was better known by his nom de plume, George Orwell. Little did my grandparents realise, but he was about to embark on arguably the greatest work of fiction of the 20th century, the totalitarian nightmare, *1984*.

Sixty-three years later, sitting in the very same farmhouse, the shadow of Orwell and his achievements still looms large. Indeed, grainy pictures of the author himself adorn the spartan walls and, while the peaceful setting could hardly feel further removed from his dystopian vision, the legacy of Orwell's brief sojourn is palpable and has had a huge influence on the lives of the Fletcher family, including myself.

My parents inherited the cottage when I was only ten and I initially failed to grasp the true significance of either the writer or his work. Yet as I spent more time on Jura, I was amazed to find a string of people appearing to peer in the window of our lonely abode.

These pilgrims, who would brave rain, wind and midges aplenty as they trudged up the five miles of the same rutted track that my grandparents' van had once taken, clearly saw Orwell as some sort of literary saint. While some of the visitors have been rude and invasive – barging into the house unannounced and unwelcome – others, such as the Japanese professor who arrived with only a tail-coat and patent leather shoes to ward off a storm, have earned their share of whatever meagre resources I can muster from a fridge-less building that is two hours from a shop. While I'd read the book on numerous occasions, it was this string of visitors and discussions about Orwell that made me truly appreciate the difference he had made to the lives of people all over the world. And, without a doubt, *1984* has since made a huge impact on my life too, partially through absorbing its bleak indictment of a totalitarian state and partially because the book acted as a gateway to the rest of his writing – I have since earned an MA in history, courtesy of my knowledge of Orwell's work. However, quite uniquely, it is also thanks to its association with Jura that I have since shared a cup of tea and a roll-up round Orwell's erstwhile table with contemporary journalists and writers, such as Will Self.

SIMON FRASER'S STORY

Superman: From the '30s to the '70s

by Jerry Siegle and Joe Shuster

SYNOPSIS

An anthology of Superman stories, from his inception by Siegle and Shuster up until his 1970s heyday being drawn by Curt Swan. With an introduction by E. Nelson Bridwell

MY STORY

I was given this book when I was maybe nine years old. I have an aunt who had very insightful taste in Christmas presents. This one was her triumph, bearing in mind my subsequent career as a comics artist. I've maybe read this book over 100 times in the course of my life. It's at once comforting and inspiring. It's a child's power fantasy, raw escapism (and some of the early stuff is very raw), it's the dream of a brighter, more optimistic new world. Superman is the embodiment of an ideal – power guided by altruism. His greatest superpower perhaps is the ability to discern what the right thing to do is. X-ray vision maybe, but also great clarity of vision. The best Superman stories weren't about solving problems with his fists, but with his imagination, and occasionally some very lateral thinking. The very best Superman stories were about ideas. Not dogma and not politics, but perhaps a little religious.

The modern world has endlessly reworked and regurgitated these original ideas until all that's left is a garish kind of cultural toxic-waste. The whole comics medium was an embarrassing ghetto for decades as the fan boys took over the industry and made more and more ludicrous and violent iterations of that one original idea. The greatest superhero of them all still manages to sit apart from it though and this book shows us why.

My original paperback copy is now hopelessly dog-eared and I've bought a hardback replacement. I can't bear to get rid of the original though, so they sit side by side on my shelf and always will.

JANICE GALLOWAY'S STORY
Piano Course; Book A (The Red Book)
by John W. Schaum

SYNOPSIS

A comprehensive piano tutor series for beginners of all ages. Well presented with colour pictures, useful information and guidance material.

MY STORY

When I was 11, the family, against every calculable odd, acquired a second-hand upright piano. It was a nice piece of furniture, but my mother saw the main drawback within minutes: somebody would want to play it. And that means money for lessons. The somebody, of course, was me. I'd seen Liberace on TV and I wanted, passionately, to play.

Miss Hughes, who lived in a sheltered flat with paper-thin walls, took me on, and that was when we acquired it: the John W. Schaum *Piano Course, Book A (The Red Book)* 'Leading to Mastery of the Instrument in Easy Steps'. Despite the seven bob (35p) price-tag, my mother bought it. The book had a red baby grand on the cover; its first page was blank with an instruction to draw around your own hands and number the fingers, one to five. A flick through the rest showed tests, tips and interesting facts ('A mazurka is a Polish Dance') and – joy! – little drawings with each eight-bar tune to colour in, once the piece had been learned. I remember in particular the welcome page from Mr Schaum, an American stranger, wishing me, some anonymous Scottish nobody, 'Good Luck and years of happy playing!' because it moved me to tears.

I still have the drawing of the hands, the tests with answers in my 11-year-old script. There are my first terms – lento, allegro, mysterioso; the thick five-line stave with coin-like empty note-heads containing their single-letter names. I remember looking at those letters, drawing round them with one finger. This book was a pencil outline of the map to Another World. It would teach me music.

My mother had hoped for Lerner and Loewe show tunes requiring Grade Six. What she got was 'The Wood-Chuck', 'The Little Elf', and a beautifully simplified 'Nutcracker'. She got more in due time. And I have kept the Schaum. I know it was no great shakes – more 'Baseball Song' and 'Hoedown!' than the snippets of Chopin and Mozart and Bach I learned to love. But they were first steps. They led to free lessons at secondary school, the orchestra, the Purcell and Britten that caught my imagination and changed my life. My first piano primer gave me a language of only seven letters, yet containing every sound imaginable. Mr Schaum, Miss Hughes and mum, thanks.

DIANA SOFIA GAMIO'S STORY
Tuesdays with Morrie
by Mitch Albom

SYNOPSIS

This is the story of Mitch's last days with his old college professor and friend Morrie who is dying from a form of motor neurone disease (ALS). Morrie is an amazing, inspirational and wise man who teaches Mitch about what really matters in life.

MY STORY

I read this book recently and I completely fell in love with it. I really felt as if Morrie was teaching me about life rather than teaching Mitch. I could connect with Morrie's aphorisms and felt uplifted by his warm words of wisdom.

At the time that I read this book, I was going through a bit of a rough time. I had broken up with my boyfriend who was also my best guy friend and I felt as if all my friendships were falling apart. I was becoming too wrapped up in the fact that my relationship with him had ended because of no apparent reason and found myself constantly thinking about things related to him. It seemed as if I had no time to spend with my family or the people who truly cared about me; but this book was my wake-up call. It helped me remember that regret is irrelevant in life where as forgiveness and love are everything. I realised once again, that making the most of now was necessary and that I could be surrounded by love without having my ex-boyfriend around. I remembered that it is important to give people chances – as many as they need, but I cannot physically change them.

I simply love this book.

MARTIN GILLESPIE'S STORY

It

by Stephen King

SYNOPSIS

It is a novel about childhood, about friendships and fears, a meditation on lost innocence that transcends its horror conventions.

MY STORY

I read this book in 1987, soon after its publication. I was 13. My English teacher, a huge Stephen King fan, gave me her copy to read. When I eventually finished it – it is by any standards a huge book – I felt that I had read the greatest novel ever written. I no longer feel that way, but for reasons that seem to resonate with time, I find myself wondering if my teacher realised how affecting her simple generosity would prove.

More than a horror novel, *It* is about friendship, about the nature of memory, how key events in our childhood shape the people we become. By exploring the relationships of the children, and the adversity that brings them together, it draws a touching picture of the worries and complexities of youth.

I was a similar age to the main characters when I read the book and I found King's remote view of what I myself was experiencing painfully accurate. His appreciation for the fleeting moments of youth gave me pause to consider my time in a way no dry grown-up adage could. 'These are the best years of your life.' Really?

His heroes had emotional depth. They embodied every possible reason for alienation; religious, physical, intellectual, psychological. They were the self-proclaimed 'loser's club'. A group who ultimately triumphed, both as children, and as adults, when they were called upon to relive the terrible events in which they could no longer believe.

It changed something in me. It gave me hope, a licence to dream, as well as a buffer for my own social shortcomings. Now, when I think back, I remember a time of encroaching responsibilities, of exams and career choices, and a novel that let me believe in magic a little longer.

CAMILLA GORDON'S STORY
Noughts and Crosses
by Malorie Blackman

SYNOPSIS

A novel set in an imagined segregated world where white people are the social underclass. This plot follows two people who are in love with each other but encounter difficulties, prejudice and persecution because they are from different racial backgrounds.

MY STORY

This book changed my life, in that it was one of the first books I read which actually made me think about the world in which we live and how we interact with the people around us. This book is about racism, looking at how the world would be if white people had been scorned and segregated with black people being in control. It looks at so many things which we take for granted today that have been fought for over many years. The moment which sticks in my mind is when we see a 'Nought' (white girl) sitting in a school for 'Crosses' (black children), eating lunch with a black plaster on her head. She gets asked why she has a black plaster on such a white head, and responds that no white plasters are made. This made a profound impression on me, thinking about how something so simple yet so essential could be overlooked or someone could even be scorned because of something like this. It was this book that impressed on me the fact that there is no place for racism or any kind of bullying anywhere in this world and taught me about how important it is to listen to other people and work together to solve problems rather than fighting each other to make our voices heard.

CHRISTINA GORRIE'S STORY
Daffodils
by William Wordsworth

SYNOPSIS

A collection of poems featuring one of Wordsworth's best known poems 'Daffodils' with its famous opening line 'I wandered lonely as a cloud...'

MY STORY

I was at secondary school in my early teens and having English lessons from my teacher, Mr Proctor. At the end of the lesson he told the class to learn the poem by Wordsworth off by heart as our homework for the following week. I did manage to memorise the poem and was also able to stand up in class and recite it in front of everyone. This was not a simple task for me as I lacked confidence and always blushed the colour of beetroot when asked to do anything like this.

This reddening of my face was very embarrassing. When anything went wrong in class and we were asked who did it, my face always went red and the teachers would think I was the guilty party.

One holiday in 1967 my boyfriend and I went for a run in his car, as we often did in those days, when the roads were quieter and going out in the car was very enjoyable. We made our way up the A9 in Perthshire and stopped in Aberfeldy for a look around the gift shops and had a bite to eat. We then continued our journey towards a beautiful village by Loch Tay called Kenmore. We turned a corner and there they were. On each side of a driveway leading up to a big house, fluttering and dancing in the breeze our very own sight, a host of golden daffodils. All at once I started to recite Wordsworth's poem to the amazement of my boyfriend. He was impressed and later proposed to me. I said yes and can honestly say seeing the daffodils and reciting the poem changed my life. Now our garden in the spring time hosts many golden daffodils and I now enjoy writing poetry to catch these special moments and put them into words.

JENNI GREEN'S STORY
Swallows and Amazons
by Arthur Ransome

SYNOPSIS

A children's novel in which a group of children have adventures sailing and camping in the Lake District in August 1929. In the process, the intrepid explorers meet Amazon pirates and the retired Captain Flint, go whaling, dig for buried treasure, eat pemmican and drink lots of grog.

MY STORY

I was a bit slow to develop as a child. I talked late; I crawled late; I didn't walk until I was three. Doctors spent months prodding my hips in case there was something wrong with them and prodding my mind in case there was something wrong with it.

And I came to reading late as well. A couple of years after starting school, I could read and I wasn't a stupid child, but I refused point-blank to read to myself for pleasure. I loved stories, could never get enough of them, but at the same age my sisters had already read their way through Enid Blyton and were tackling *Anne of Green Gables*, whilst I was still insisting that my mother read to me every night.

Mum was losing her voice and losing her patience. She took *Swallows and Amazons* off the shelf and read to 'the exciting bit' before putting the book down for the night. I pleaded with her to keep reading. She refused. She informed me in no uncertain terms that if I wanted to know what happened next, I would have to read it myself.

There may have been a tantrum that first night. But she did the same thing the following night, and the next, and within a fortnight her cunning plan had worked.

I devoured the rest of the series whole, straining my eyes reading with a torch under the duvet; then, when I ran out of Arthur Ransome, I hit the library, discovered Susan Cooper and never looked back.

I live my life these days with a book constantly in my hand, still getting as much pleasure out of each new story as I did then; but every year or two, I still re-read all the *Swallows and Amazons* books. Every time, I find something new in them. They're so beautifully crafted; lyrical in description, real in feeling. The characters are vivid, unique, three-dimensional, but still recognisably children; I envied the fun they were having but identified with all the fears and insecurities that seem so much bigger when you're ten.

As a girl, I also appreciated Ransome's gender politics; books where girls were in the majority, where they were allowed to be girls but still got to do whatever the boys did (and did not feature ballet, ponies or boarding schools) were pretty rare in my limited experience.

I grew up with those characters, in the Lakes and on the Broads, and they've influenced my childhood and my adult life to a huge extent. If I had been born 15 years later it might have been Harry Potter and I might be a very different person.

A couple of years ago, I made up a poster of inspirational quotes from the books, which still hangs over my desk and reminds me every day to 'Never say dee til ye're deid'.

ROBBIE HANDY'S STORY
Portrait of a Young Man Drowning
by Charles Perry

SYNOPSIS

Harry Odum struggles for survival in 1940s Brooklyn. His social awkwardness, absentee father and oedipal relationship with his mother, lead him to seek solace in the arms of the Brooklyn Mafia. Harry befriends Abie the Bug, an assassin who trains him in the black arts. As Harry moves up the ranks, he is forced to take a terrible decision which sees him spiral into bloodlust and insanity.

MY STORY

When Ah wis 17, Ah'd just left school. Ah wis disillusioned wi education an felt socially isolated. Ah wis expected tae go tae university, but after a breakdown, Ah left school an entered a world o pimps, fast women, drugs an murder. Ma soundtrack wis hip-hop, soul an reggae. Readin books like *Pimp* by Iceberg Slim an *Portrait of A Young Man Drowning*, Ah escaped fae the monotony o life in 1990s Fife. Ma escape wisnae intae a world o wizards, millionaire playboys or superheroes, but intae the killing fields an crack dens o Baltimore, Brooklyn an South Central.

The title wis what first attracted me tae Perry's book, as Ah felt that Ah wis slowly drownin maself, starved o stimulation an options, descendin intae a mental vortex. Ah wis surprised when Ah got intae it though. Perry wis a black writer, an because o racism, chose tae set his story in the white world o the Brooklyn Mafia. The dialogue is sharp an brutal, infused wi gallows humor that would put *Goodfellas* tae shame. Harry's naïveté is exploited by the hoods, but his bloodlust is fuelled by rage at his social ineptitude, twisted relationships with women, an lack o family support. He takes tae his new trade like a duck tae a bloodstained loch.

The characters, dialogue an descriptions brough me right there, tae the streets o Brooklyn, on the pavement outside the old garage where the hitmen take their orders an then bring the bodies back tae chop up. However, there's loads o Mafia tales, an we're so numbed by overexposure that characters like Tony Soprano become lovable rogues, their violence is banal, diluted by humour an glamour.

What really shocked me about Perry's book wis his visceral descriptions o Harry's bloody descent tae insanity. As Ah read it, Ah escaped tae the more familiar Mafia world, but wis quickly trapped in the extra-dimensional liminality o Harry's mind, as his psychosis blooms an erupts, an his family, friends an colleagues aw become legitimate targets for his insensate rage.

The book blew ma mind. As ye kin guess, it disnae have a happy endin. What it showed me though, wis the power o the word, the force o imagination. Perry abandons syntax an form, sentences read backwards, forwards, words reel in loops an fly off the page as mental torment consumes Harry. Bullets an bodies bounce off the paper an intae yer mind.

The book didnae depress me though, it inspired me. It wis a middle finger up tae the world. Ah realised that Ah could start tae write ma way out ma own problems, wi imagination an determination. So, Ah'm sure the end tae ma story will be happier than Harry's. Mebbe some o ma old teachers'll read this. If they do, here's a middle finger tae them!

CAROLINE HENLEY'S STORY
The Boy with the Bronze Axe
by Kathleen Fidler

SYNOPSIS

A Scottish children's adventure story set in the Stone Age in Skara Brae on Orkney, in which two children encounter a strange boy who brings with him an axe made of a very strange substance. His presence changes life in the village forever, although it's about to be changed even further by the approach of a deadly storm.

MY STORY

I was just starting school when my older brother came home with this as his class reader. He wasn't very keen on reading at that time so my mum would read along with him.

We all became hooked on this book and would look forward to reading more. It was really difficult to stick to reading the chapter at a time the class had been given as homework!

My class weren't given the book as one of our readers when I got to the same age three years later but I did borrow it and mum and I both read it again. When I first qualified as a librarian I found the book on the shelf at library headquarters and we both read it for a third time – it hadn't lost any of its magic!

Sadly we lost mum at the start of this year but I'll never forget the excitement of sharing that wonderful story together and how it hooked me on reading for life.

I wish she'd lived long enough so we could have visited Skara Brae together but I will do it one day and I know she'll be with me.

GRANT JOHNSON'S STORY
The Easy Way to Stop Smoking
by Allen Carr

SYNOPSIS

This book is a self-help guide to quitting smoking. Being an ex-smoker the author deals with nicotine addiction and its withdrawal symptoms from his own experience, taking the reader on a journey to their last cigarette.

MY STORY

I discovered this book a few years ago, from a cousin at a family wedding reception. I offered him a cigarette and he refused and our conversation turned to the subject of the addictive habit. My cousin Gordon answered that he had given up with the help of a book, and asked me if I wanted to stop. I immediately answered yes. He asked why I was so sure, and I mentioned an incident that occurred a few weeks prior to the wedding.

I had returned to work after a period of inactivity due to a leg injury, during which I spent resting, drinking endless cups of tea and coffee, and smoking numerous fags. I rolled my own so I couldn't keep an accurate count, but it was a lot more than usual. I was cycling home after my first shift for over two weeks and I built up a bit of speed on the flat in order to combat a hill that normally, I managed in the saddle. This time however, my breathing became erratic. I quickly lost my rhythm with the gears, causing me to dismount. I was coughing, spitting and through the spots before my eyes, I lost my pride and dignity before what seemed a huge crowd magnifying my self-inflicted predicament. In fact it was only a few people waiting for a bus that I walked meekly past.

I recovered enough to cycle the rest of the way home realising that I would have to seriously address my smoking problem. Since then I had been conscious of every cigarette and was trying to cut down.

On hearing this, Gordon agreed, and said that it was probably the right time for me to read the book. The right time being a time when I was wishing that I could kick the habit but I lacked conviction, self belief and, the main stumbling block from previous attempts, I suffered from the fear of failure.

Gordon, who stayed in London, sent me a copy from a large bookstore there (one of the few outlets at that time).

Although I didn't stop instantly, I instantly related to the author and somehow sensed that, with the help of this book, I would eventually give up smoking. He is an ex-smoker himself and has therefore experienced the difficulties concerned with trying to stop. He covers all aspects related to the subject in a most understanding and effective manner. It's coming up for 20 years since I became one of his high success rates, and overcame my fear of failure to proudly become a much fitter, healthier and happier non-smoker

A.L. KENNEDY'S STORY

The Restaurant at the End of the Universe

by Douglas Adams

SYNOPSIS

This second volume in the *Hitchhiker's Guide to the Galaxy* series is definitely not a standalone book. In it, we enjoy the continuing adventures of Earthling Arthur Dent, his strange pal Ford Prefect, and the very, very odd Zaphod Beeblebrox.

MY STORY

I'm going to be slightly embarrassed about this – and I'd have to emphasise that I read all kinds of books when I was kid, devoured them, and all of them did me the world of good a multiplicity of ways. But if I think of one that was exceptionally timely and helpful the first that comes to mind is *The Restaurant at the End of the Universe* by Douglas Adams. It doesn't contain the greatest prose ever – although it is musical, Adams had a great ear – and the humour can be slightly formulaic, but that book did save my mental bacon.

When I was in my early teens I had a minor health problem which involved my first contact with doctors I hadn't met before as cosy family practitioners, examinations I had never dreamed of, massive, long-corridored hospitals and a whole panoply of mildly panicky and threatening consultations – a contact with science that seemed to do nothing to assist my health and everything to leave me with a sense of bizarrely random prodding and adult incompetence.

I happened to be going through a sci-fi phase at the time and, as far as was possible, I folded myself away from whatever medical procedure happened to be happening and imagined myself as Zaphod Beeblebrox – a character I never did actually warm to much under any other circumstances. Zaphod was, of course, dragged into the Total Perspective Vortex and forced to confront his almost infinite smallness in the face of reality – something which was usually fatal. The Vortex was silly enough and horrible enough to be just the place for my mind to hide away in and I am grateful to it to this day.

And I have retained my fondness for sci-fi, too.

JARED KROPP-THIERRY'S STORY

The Sopranos

by Alan Warner

SYNOPSIS

A group of Scottish Catholic schoolgirls go to the big city to take part in a national choir competition. The sopranos of the choir decide to use this opportunity to let loose and enjoy the freedom of being in a big city. They get themselves into all sorts of troubles that reveal how much of life they have still to learn about. Far more important than the competition, the girls are anxious to get back to their home town, as a group of submariners are arriving from a nuclear sub.

MY STORY

I read *The Sopranos* when I was just 15 years old and it made a huge impact. As a shy and sensitive teenager, I knew nothing of women's ways or about drinking and sex and getting into discos underage. *The Sopranos* opened up a whole new perspective on how teenage girls interacted and thought about things. This is odd in a way, as it was written by a man in his '30s, but everything in the book rang so true and each character seemed like a person I could actually meet in my own home town. These complicated young women on the cusp of adulthood were enjoying their youth whilst also dealing with their fears of the future. I was the same age as them and it made me realise that perhaps boys and girls were not so different. The fact that they clearly had desires and enjoyed getting drunk felt like a revelation to me. It was exciting to get an inside look into what girls actually talked about when they went to the toilets together. This book also presented an often raw but also compassionate insight into teenage behaviour. The girls get drunk and have sex without precaution but you understand why they might be so excessive and darn right stupid. These are lower working-class girls who have few opportunities beyond school and they know it. When they go to the city, they act all tough but inside are terrified and unsure. This was exactly how I felt when I went to see my older friend at university when I was 15 years old. This book helped me see that I was not alone and that girls also had fears and insecurities. They might act all confident and dismissive but perhaps they were as worried about what I thought about them as I was about how they viewed me. It was the book that made me see the similarities between the genders and realise that being a teenager is hard regardless of whether you are a boy or a girl.

KENNY LOGAN'S STORY
Lassie Come-Home
by Eric Knight and Rosemary Wells

SYNOPSIS

When Sam Carraclough falls on hard times, he is forced to sell his prize collie to a wealthy family. But Lassie, although she is taken hundreds of miles away, knows it is her duty to meet young Joe from school – so she starts on the long and difficult journey home.

MY STORY

I was 16 years old when I read a book for the first time. It was *Lassie*, written for nine-year-olds. It wasn't until I left school that dyslexia was first mentioned.

I had walked out on my exams without being able to write a word. The supervisor had intercepted me but I told him, 'I can't read. I can't even write my address. There's nothing for me here.'

My mother arranged for me to go round to a teacher, Deirdre Wilson's house once or twice a week after I'd left school and I did this for about a year. It was Deirdre who was the first to diagnose me with dyslexia. It was a great relief to know what the problem had been – even that there had been a problem at all – but it was frustrating, knowing all I could do was keep trying.

I went through *Lassie* word by word, and after a page I was exhausted. I just couldn't take any of it in. Deirdre was fantastic, and I'll always be grateful for the effort she put in. The whole experience was a positive change in my life, because now I had a reason and a word for my troubles with reading: dyslexia. But I soon realised that there was no quick solution and the endless struggle to get round, or just to cover up, my illiteracy was going to continue.

From the moment I met my wife Gabby I knew my life had changed. She sussed me out almost immediately. Not only that, but she could see what dyslexia had done to me and what it might still go on to do. She pushed and pushed and pushed until I'd faced up to my condition, the guilty secret and bane of my life, until I had finally done something about it. I finally learnt those vowels, aged 30. Anything seemed possible.

KIRSTY LOGAN'S STORY
Horrible Histories
by Terry Deary

SYNOPSIS

Horrible Histories is a long-running series of children's history books 'with the nasty bits left in'. The books are broken down into little chunks of cartoons, snippets and stories that range from the repulsive to the inane. Each has an alliterative title, like *The Angry Aztecs*, *The Groovy Greeks*, *The Rotten Romans*, and *The Villainous Victorians*.

MY STORY

I am a lazy intellectual, an academic slacker, a dilettante who likes to know a little bit about everything. I love to learn things, but I hate to read textbooks. Adults can't be all that different from their childish counterparts, because I've always been that way.

Every six months between the ages of eight and 12, my teacher handed out book catalogues from a mail-order company. I'd circle at least half the books with my pencil and take the catalogue home to my parents. The only ones my father would buy me were the *Horrible Histories* – I guess he thought that books on history must surely be educational. Little did he know that they were full of blood, gore, violence, and dirty jokes.

That's not to say that they weren't educational. I cried at the Victorian women in the mines, forced to crawl on their knees, harnessed to the heavy coal carts. I laughed at the slang from the 1960s, the 1800s and the 1660s. I looked sceptically at my mother's make-up after learning that Georgian women beautified themselves with belladonna eye-drops that made them blind and lead face-powder that leached poison into their skin. I obsessed over the Aztec sacrifices of adolescents, their bodies piled high in bloody pits. I had nightmares about the Roman fisherman who trekked across the country to offer a fish to the Emperor, who decreed it too small and ordered the man to be skinned with the scales of the fish. I played the same games as children in the First World War.

I had always liked reading stories, but before *Horrible Histories* I hadn't realised that interesting stories could be true.

I think it's safe to say that almost everything I know about history I learned from *Horrible Histories* books. They've got me through school essays and pub quizzes – I sometimes even get a few questions right when watching University Challenge.

CAROLINE MacAFEE'S STORY

A Dictionary of the Older Scottish Tongue

by William Craigie

SYNOPSIS

A multi-volume historical dictionary, considered an authoritative reference work on the Scots language up to the year 1700.

MY STORY

The book that gave me a lifelong love of scholarship was a dictionary. When I first came across *A Dictionary of the Older Scottish Tongue* (DOST), I was a student at the University of Edinburgh, where it was still being edited and published, one fascicle at a time. On the shelves of the university library, where I often consulted it for essays on the Scots language, only the first three volumes were bound. The senior editor, Jack Aitken, also taught English Language, and that is how it came about that, as a mere third year student, I was able to make a contribution to the dictionary.

I found a word. I don't remember now what it was, but it was new to the dictionary. I found it when I was given the task – for a mere undergraduate essay – of transcribing a couple of pages of a manuscript not at that time available in a modern edition. I was sent, with a letter of introduction, to the National Library of Scotland. I felt wonderfully privileged to be allowed in, and even more so when the manuscript that I asked for was brought to me. Later, when I went to collect my marked essay from Jack Aitken, in his office at the dictionary, I was entranced by the scale of the operation, the eident staff, and the banks of pigeonholes full of dictionary slips.

When I learned that my contribution was to be used – at face value, with no further checking by anybody else – I felt a mixture of awe and responsibility that I can only compare to the first time I was allowed to hold a baby. Or to put it another way, for a moment I had been handed the baton of scholarship and allowed to take a step with it.

IAN MacFARLANE'S STORY

The Mists of Avalon

by Marion Zimmer Bradley

SYNOPSIS

A retelling of the Arthurian legend told through the lives of the ladies of Camelot. A bewitching tale of love, betrayal and an idealistic dream doomed to fail.

MY STORY

Moving house. Filling boxes. Discovering long lost memories, stored away in the darkest corners of cupboards... darkest corners of my mind. A bookmark falls out of a book, a photo of a beautiful young girl on a pony. On the back are the words, 'I hope you like this as much as I do.'

I have only read *The Mists of Avalon* once. I have been scared to read it again. I was 19, she was 17. I was so much in love, my first love. I told her as much knowing she might never utter the words. She was too perfect, too free-spirited to weigh herself down with such heavy words. Seasons blurred and youthful emotions grew strong and bold. We promised each other the world, everlasting dreams of romance and naïve hope. I thought it was impossible to be any happier. I was wrong.

'I want to give you something', she said.

I could see she was nervous, fidgeting in that adorable way, knowing she was fighting to defeat her weak, treacherous emotions.

I had to promise I would not open it until I was alone. When I did, I discovered the book and the photo. I had always believed books to be an individual pursuit, not to be shared with others – mix-tapes were how we conveyed our confused feelings. Again, I was wrong.

I stayed awake for hours, desperately looking for hidden messages within the text, signs of her undying love for me. Yet somewhere in the mists of reading, I discovered a world of love and magic which made me forget my own quest. A world full of hurt, betrayal and darkness and yet balanced by a sense of hope, dreams and of legends come to life. The strong female characters, so believable in this land of myth, all seemed to encapsulate in some way the girl I loved. And now I understood. She truly loved me. She had bared her soul by allowing me into this world. No medley of songs could ever have produced the understanding and bond that this book created.

'I love you so much,' she told me two weeks later.

'I know.' Unlike Camelot we would be together forever. No sorcery would be able to break our love...

I have not seen her in years. My first love. The mists of time have healed all the pain and heartache. I pack all my books in boxes, to be hidden away for another ten years. Except one. I pass the book to my beautiful wife. 'I think you might like this.'

I thought it was impossible to be any happier. I was wrong.

ANN MacLAREN'S STORY
Heidi
by Johanna Spyri

SYNOPSIS

A classic children's novel telling the story of Heidi, a small girl who lives with her grandfather in his little wooden house high up in the mountains of Switzerland. One day Heidi's aunt arrives and takes her to Clara's home in Frankfurt. Heidi likes her new friend, but she doesn't like living in a big house in the city. Together she and Clara learn about friendship, sacrifice and courage.

MY STORY

I was seven before I owned my first book, given to me as a First Prize for General Excellence from Rosemount Primary School in Roystonhill, Glasgow. My previous reading material had been confined to school books and the occasional comic, but I was a competent reader and it took me no time at all to devour the story of Heidi – a story which told of a little girl of about my own age, living with her grandfather in a wooden chalet in the mountains, playing with her friends in the clean fresh air of the Swiss Alps, eating chunks of homemade bread with delicious cheese, drinking creamy milk fresh from the goats and sleeping in a soft bed made of straw.

Heidi's idyllic environment was so different from my own that I shouldn't have been able to identify with it at all: my life was a dirty grey inner city tenement, a bad-tempered father, a Milanda pan loaf with shop jam, sugary tea and a bed shared with my brother and sister. I knew a bit about mountains though. We had mountains in Glasgow, just down the road from where I lived. Mountains of rubbish. And when I was a child it was the best place in the world to go on a summer evening. Dozens of us played there, ignoring the warnings of our parents who tried to frighten us with tales of scarlet fever and tetanus and diphtheria as we searched around in the muck and dust for a discarded toy or a 'lucky' (anything from a colourful piece of glass to an unusual stone could be a lucky, you just had to announce it in a loud voice). We would build dens and castles, choose leaders, split into Cowboys and Indians, have battles and generally rule the world.

My mountains were not like Heidi's, but the description of that other way of life in those Swiss Alps, green and lush, snow-capped but bathed in sunshine, kept me reading. I was there. I was Heidi. I walked up the long steep path to Grandfather's house, played in the long grass, helped Peter with his goats and held Clara's hand as she made her first tentative steps away from her wheelchair.

It took me many years to understand the sadness I felt when I turned the last page of the book and the story, fully resolved and with every character life-affirmingly happy, came to an end. That sense of loss, of not wanting the story to end, led me to other books – by way of a membership ticket at Townhead Library where I was allowed to borrow not one, but two, books. Every week! Since reading *Heidi*, I've never been without a book – or a library membership.

DREW MacLELLAN'S STORY
DK Dinosaur Encyclopaedia
by Carolyn Bingham

SYNOPSIS

DK Dinosaur Encyclopaedia is an illustrated book for children full of facts, figures and pictures to teach children about dinosaurs.

MY STORY

This book didn't change my life, but the life of my son. We found out that he was on the autistic spectrum when he was three years old and didn't really understand what to do. He wasn't engaged by television programmes, he didn't like socialising and he didn't start speaking until very late on. We didn't know how we could help him and his behaviour was often difficult. One day I was at the library with Ritchie and I picked up this book to let him look at the pictures. So began his burning obsession with dinosaurs! We borrowed the book from the library and he read it non-stop until he knew every fact about every type of dinosaur. It was fantastic to see him so excited and engaged with something – we found him more books about dinosaurs and bought him his own copy of the *DK Dinosaur Encyclopaedia*. He now knows so much about dinosaurs he could probably write his own book. For us, this was a revelation. We found out that it was common for boys with ASD to form obsessions with things like dinosaurs, trains or other fact-rich topics because it helps them to make sense of the world. We realised that there are a lot of little boys out there who speak in an American accent and don't like to be hugged. We found that our son was incredibly bright in his own way and that we should respect his way of doing things. So in a way this book changed all our lives.

ALEXANDER McCALL SMITH'S STORY
Collected Shorter Poems
by W.H. Auden

SYNOPSIS

In his lifetime a controversial, outspoken, yet enigmatic writer, W.H. Auden was once described as the Picasso of modern poetry. This volume is an introduction to the craftsmanship and originality which made him the master-poet of his generation.

MY STORY

The single book that changed my view of the world more than any other book is W.H. Auden's *Collected Shorter Poems*. It may be unusual for a book of poetry to have this effect, but such is the power and range of Auden's genius that this collection of poems written between 1927 and 1957 quite simply opened my eyes. I remember the precise moment I first encountered it. I was a young man and I picked it off a library shelf on impulse. I took the book out and began to read it. Somehow it seemed that Auden was talking directly to me, that I was in the presence of a most marvellous, humane intelligence.

Auden was a poet who used almost every metre available. His was one of the most complex and accomplished literary minds of the 20th century and his feel for the English language and its lyrical possibilities was unrivalled in the poets of his generation.

His work reads effortlessly, but has great technical skill behind it. And his choice of subjects is extraordinarily wide: love, science, geology, opera, history, politics – in fact, there is little in our human experience that Auden does not cover. In this collection we see him change – from the poet who believed in the perfectibility of man through social change, to the poet who had to come to terms with inherent and incorrigible evil.

This book contains some of his very greatest work. 'Limestone Landscape', one of his best-known poems, tells of his love-affair with a particular sort of countryside; 'In Memory of Sigmund Freud' dwells on the liberating power of psychoanalytical insights; and then there is the simple gravity of 'Lullaby', perhaps the most powerful hymn to carnal love ever written: 'Lay your sleeping head my love...'

Auden's words are a constant source of inspiration to me. In one of my books, *The Comfort of Saturdays*, I wrote about a lecture being delivered by W.H. Auden's literary executor, the distinguished critic Professor Edward Mendelson. I then invited Professor Mendelson to Edinburgh to deliver the lecture which he gives in this book, thereby making fiction a reality.

He wrote the poem 'Musée des Beaux-Arts' – about how extraordinary things happen while people are simply getting on with their business. The poem in question deals with Brueghel's depiction of the fall of Icarus; the boy falls from the sky while a farmer ploughs his fields, a horse scratches its rump against a tree, and a ship gets on with its voyage. He was right. People carry on with their lives even if something important is going on under their noses.

I carry this book around with me on my travels. I never tire of dipping into it and finding something new. It never fades. It is in no sense diminished by the passage of time. A constant companion.

ANDREW McCALLUM'S STORY

Linmill Stories

by Robert McLellan

SYNOPSIS

Scottish playwright and poet McLellan shares his favourite childhood memories in this collection of stories. Set on and around Linmill Farm, where the author was born and spent many summer holidays, this collection is a beautifully-crafted evocation of a childhood spent in the fertile Clyde Valley in the early 20th century.

MY STORY

My mother gave me *Linmill Stories* to read in the late 1970s when I was in my early '20s. She liked it mainly because, being a Clydesdale lass, she was amused by the local references; but also because it spoke to her powerfully of her own life experience as a girl growing up as the daughter of an itinerant farm labourer, in a succession of ferm touns where Scots was still the living language outside the school and the kirk.

I had given up speaking Scots because my family was working class and my mother thought that I should speak only Proper English; yet among themselves my parents and grandparents, aunts and uncles and neighbours all spoke Scots, with the result that I understood the language perfectly but was unable to speak it.

Then I read *Linmill Stories* and, all of a sudden, from the cavern of my throat, the tongue grew; so that now when I go to see my mother I can speak to her, naturally, in her own language. The stories were authentic, unsentimental; a million miles from the kailyaird and the self-mockery of music-hall Scotch and the romantic mythologies of tartan nationalism. They were serious literature – Clyde Valley Chekhov – and they validated my mother's tongue as a serious literary language. The speik was nothing to be ashamed of. It was something other and greater than the degenerate form of English employed by coorse tinks and tartan clowns that I had been led to believe it was.

As well as the courtly dance that is a conversation with my mother in Scots, I write. I write in Scots as well as English; not because I have any great desire to preserve a language that passed with the things that seemed good to my parents' and grandparents' generation, 'with loves and desires that grow dim and alien in the days to be', nor because I feel any need to assert in my discourse a distinctive national identity that will mark me off from those of other tribes, but simply because there are things I can say in Scots that I can't say in English. Scots is a rich linguistic resource that a poet can exploit in his or her attempts to lyric existence; and it was in Robert McLellan's *Linmill Stories* that I first discovered this.

ROBIN McCALLUM'S STORY

1984

by George Orwell

SYNOPSIS

Hidden away in the Record Department of the sprawling Ministry of Truth, Winston Smith skilfully rewrites the past to suit the needs of the Party. Yet he inwardly rebels against the totalitarian world he lives in, which demands absolute obedience and controls him through the all-seeing telescreens and the watchful eye of Big Brother, symbolic head of the Party. In his longing for truth and liberty, Smith begins a secret love affair with a fellow-worker Julia, but soon discovers the true price of freedom is betrayal.

MY STORY

A wis fair determined no tae like or be impressed by this book but it happened anywise – agin ma will! A got it oot the local library when A wis a lad of 20 or there aboots an' A thocht everythin A'd heard aboot it wis goin tae fall flat. An o'ercooked puddin, A thocht. A wis completely wrang o' course, the idea o' a thocht police wha cud clamp doon oan yer rebellious notions wis gey terrifyin an nae sa far fae whit went oan in Stalin's Russia – ne'er mind *Animal Farm*, this wis showin' the impact sic a controlling an reactionary regime cud huv had oan the lives o it's citizens. The final betrayal wis jist an unexpectit clout tae the story – whit extremes cud a man find himsel' in when he's a lone renegade? A knew this book hud tae be ma choice fur the book that changed ma life – ne'er has ony book sine thrown sic a terrifying message in ma face in sic a powerful way.

MARTIN McGALE'S STORY
A Clockwork Orange
by Anthony Burgess

SYNOPSIS

Burgess employs an invented language in this depiction of a troubled teenager and his love for gang violence in a dystopian future, where a sinister government struggles to keep order against a rising tide of gang crime.

MY STORY

When I read *A Clockwork Orange* as a teenager, it was the first book that really made me think about things outside of the story itself; about society and humanity. Not only that – it made me question these things. Are we born or conditioned to be good or bad? Who gets to decide who is good and who is bad? How do we even define 'good' and 'bad'? It is also a vivid and astonishingly accurate vision of the future that was to come: gangs of teenagers owning the streets, free to roam around conducting senseless acts of violence with no remorse and no real worry of being punished – Burgess was practically describing Britain in the 2000s, 40 years before it happened. The young characters even have their own street language, which is another element that takes the book to another level. What starts off as indecipherable nonsense on page one becomes your second language by the final chapter. For its creativity with language, incredible imagery and for really making me think, *A Clockwork Orange* is the best book I have ever read.

OISIN McGANN'S STORY
The Lord of the Rings
by J.R.R. Tolkien

SYNOPSIS

A trilogy fantasy set in mythical Middle Earth, where some small human-like Hobbits embark on a life-changing journey to save their world from corruption. Assisted by the wizard Gandalf and their loyal friends, they encounter Elves, Dwarves and the horrifying Orcs, and have lots of adventures along their way.

MY STORY

I can't remember exactly what age I was when my parents introduced me to this tale. I loved the Narnia stories, but had grown out of them. I was reading Stephen King's horrors, as well as novels like *The Silver Sword*, *Watership Down* and loads of war comics. I was handed this knackered old book, the size of a brick, its pages battered, its cover held on with sellotape. I had loved *The Hobbit*, but this didn't look promising.

There was no hype around it at the time. Peter Jackson's superb films were far in the future. These books were old news – it had been out for over 20 years. There was nothing to prepare me for what I was about to read.

After the first chapter I was absolutely hooked. The four Hobbits were ordinary people thrown into a world of battle-scarred warriors and dangerous, toxic magic. Frodo was the official hero, but I preferred Sam, with his sense of humour, his loyalty and simple wisdom. Aragorn the Ranger, Legolas the Elf and Gimli the Dwarf were all hardcore. And J.K. Rowling's Dumbledore will always be a shadow of the original master wizard: Gandalf.

By today's standards, the story has some flaws. Written in a time when books didn't have to compete with games and television, there are parts of it that can seem long-winded, overly descriptive. I always skipped past the songs. There are critics who claim that *The Lord of the Rings* is not 'literature', perhaps because it has monsters, magic, strange names and so many action scenes. But can there be a difference between literature and fantastic storytelling?

The extraordinary, gritty depth of Tolkien's world, described in evocative language with superbly defined characters, humour, high drama and human detail – and loads of violent action – all combine to make this a truly awesome trilogy. I discovered it as a young boy; a story that was already decades old, wrapped in a knackered cover, its words printed on pages that were yellowing and falling from their binding. It cast a spell over me – I was desperate for the characters to succeed in their quest, but I never wanted the story to end.

This was why I wanted to write. I wanted to create stories that made people feel the way I felt when I read *The Lord of the Rings*.

SARA-JANE McGEACHY'S STORY
Tiger-Pig at the Circus
by John Ryan

SYNOPSIS

A children's story about a strange creature that doesn't fit in. Not quite a pig and not quite a tiger, our hero sets out to explore the world.

MY STORY

Tiger-Pig at the Circus came into my hands almost 30 years ago, from the distributors of great works at the Humpty-Dumpty Club, and the effect it had was profound. The story concerns a little creature whom is striped like a tiger, however (and here's the central issue for our hero), he's shaped like a pig! He goes to the circus, but is roundly rejected because of his strange appearance. By the end of the book Tiger-Pig has become a star because he looks, well, a bit odd.

Now, I don't have stripes and regardless of what others may say, I'm not shaped like a pig; but oh my Lord, I know what it's like to feel odd and rejected! I am small and rounded in stature, I have impressive scars and walk with a slight limp following an accident, I have dyed hair, tattoos and a pierced nose, I'm a Christian, an actor, a daughter and – until recently – a banker. I crave solitude and social contact in equal measure, I claim to snub popular culture, but never miss an episode of *Strictly Come Dancing*. Like every other person on the planet, I am a mass of contradictions. It's not so much a question of if I fit in, but where I fit in to.

Tiger-Pig left his parents and the little island where he lived to experience the big, wide world. He discovered that it isn't always a nice place, but ultimately, being different is a blessing not a curse. I choose to believe that Tiger-Pig met a polka-dot sow with a speech impediment and went on to have a gorgeous litter; every one of whom was completely unique. What both Tiger-Pig and I have discovered is that ordinariness is vastly overrated and we should all take time to celebrate our own peculiarity.

PAMELA McLEAN'S STORY
Not the End of the World
by Kate Atkinson

SYNOPSIS

This is a collection of short stories united by the theme of apocalypse, where classical and contemporary references are used in equal measure to explore different kinds of endings.

MY STORY

In the spring of 2003, my life was changing. I was almost at the end of my sixth and final year at school, my friends had all moved on and I was starting university after the summer. Everything familiar was ending and I felt lost.

I went to my local library at the beginning of April and browsed the adult fiction shelves. I found Kate Atkinson's book of short stories almost right away. The cover of *Not the End of the World* was gorgeous: white and gold on purple. That alone was enough to make me want to take the book home, never mind that I was already in love with the idea of the short story. But what I'd never encountered before was a piece of fiction that dealt with the world I lived in.

The world Kate Atkinson wrote about was one I recognised: Scotland; Irn-Bru; Highers; and, above all, television. I could understand references to the Buffy universe, to the mythology of *Star Trek: Voyager*. These were things I could relate to. But the worlds in all of these stories were, like my own, ending. Not everything was safe and familiar. Two stories in particular, 'Dissonance' and 'Temporal Anomaly', resonated with me because they dealt with the interruption of ordinary life for something extraordinary. I'd felt that same dislocation during the previous six months of my time at school: it came as something of a relief to see it mirrored on those pages.

The details have faded over the years and I can't claim to have reread the stories many times since then. But there are lines from that collection I will never forget, certain parts of those stories that I will always remember.

I now own a copy of the book, but the copy I first read still sits on the shelf of Partick Library. I was only the second person to take it out: you can see the due date – 3 May 2003 – stamped near the top. But the label is nearly full now, and I suppose that soon it will be torn off.

I was 17 when I read *Not the End of the World* and the stories in that collection echoed my life at the time. Had I read it at a different time, then I doubt it would have meant as much. Looking back, it was not a book that changed my life, but a book that showed me it was OK my life was changing.

ELIZABETH McNEILL'S STORY
The Horse's Mouth
by Joyce Cary

SYNOPSIS

This novel is the portrait of an impoverished painter who scorns conventional good behaviour. He may be a bad citizen, but he is a good artist. Such is his contempt for orthodox mores, he takes a delight in scorning them. For him there is only one morality: to be a painter.

MY STORY

'Here's a book that'll interest you,' said my English teacher Tom Davidson, handing me a Penguin paperback.

He had some peculiar idea that I was university material and would not accept that my ambition in life did not extend beyond winning a red ticket in the hack class at the Dublin Horse Show, but the title of his book caught my eye.

The Horse's Mouth.

And the author's name was Joyce Cary.

At least it's about a horse, and by a woman, I thought.

I was 16 and the books that made up my reading were about horses and by women with double-barrelled names like Pullein-Thomson. The heroines, Deborahs or Priscillas, entered jumping competitions and were jolly decent losers. Not like me and my brother who swore like troopers when we lost.

'At least try it,' said Tom.

I started reading on my ride home on the bus and though there was no mention of horses anywhere except in the title, I was entranced and finished it at two o'clock next morning.

I'd never heard of a man called Joyce before either, but he brought people to life on the page in a way that dazzled me and made me realise that the pony-riding heroines of my previous reading were of a class with whom I could never identify. However, I could easily visualise hanging out in a rat-ridden houseboat with Cary's anti-hero, the brilliantly named Gulley Jimson, a dissolute, drunken, disreputable artist who lived on a leaky boat on the Thames and spent his life conning people or leading them astray.

I recognised similarities between Gulley and my father Archie, for they shared the same amorality with which I sympathised, probably by genetic inheritance.

Like Gulley, Archie spent his life on the fringes of the law. He was never happy unless he was in the middle of a drama, and, as his daughter, I was often dragged into them too.

Reading Joyce Cary opened up another world for me, so wonderful and entrancing that I felt as if Tommy had taken me to a latticed gate in a stone wall and showed me a wonderful garden on the other side.

The Horse's Mouth changed my life because, if I'd never read it, I would have gone on being the co-conspirator of a horse dealer who never read anything more taxing than the *Racing Calendar* and *Horse and Hound*. Instead, because of Gulley, I went to university and started to write books myself.

Many years later I was invited to address a literary group in Edinburgh and I ran my eye over the audience looking for a friendly face.

In the back row sat Tom, almost unchanged except that his black hair had gone white.

When I told the audience that I wanted to thank him for changing my life, he stood up and said, 'You were my brand from the burning!'

ISHBEL McVICAR'S STORY
Liza of Lambeth
by William Somerset Maugham

SYNOPSIS

Liza of Lambeth was Somerset Maugham's first novel, which he wrote while working as a doctor at a hospital in Lambeth, then a working class district of London. It depicts the short life and tragic death of Liza Kemp, an 18-year-old factory worker who lives together with her aging mother in Vere Street off Westminster Bridge Road in Lambeth.

MY STORY

In 1982 I contracted Myalgic Encephalomyelitis although, at that time in the medical world, there was controversy as to what it was. 'Yuppy Flu' was one of its nicknames. After a year of back and forth to hospital, ending with a coronary artery test, it was decided if it was not my heart, then it had to be a nervous condition. I attended a consultant psychiatrist who eventually said 'Back to the physicians; it is a medical condition.' And so we moved from our home which had stairs to a cottage flat in a new district and therefore a new doctor.

My new GP asked if I read a lot and I said I used to before I was housebound. He arranged a disabled badge for me and told me to start going to the library again and to get hold of *Liza of Lambeth* and come back and tell me about it. Cognitive Behavioural Therapy it would be called nowadays. I read the book and thought I am not going like a child to tell him about it, I'll write a poem instead. I did so and here it is.

'Times Past'

Liza of Lambeth,
whose untimely death
illumines the lot
of women in an era
when life was cheap. Not
difficult to find oblivion–
at a penny a pint for gin.
The Good Old Days?

Consider, if you will,
Elizabeth of Bonhill.

The pain of bearing them
nothing to the anguish of losing them.
John died aged 6 months
Thomas died aged 9 months
Janet died aged 18 months
Mary died aged 3 years
Elizabeth died aged 6 years
Donald died aged 10 years
James died aged 12 years.
The Good Old Days?

(From a tombstone in the local churchyard.)

This led on to my writing more poems and eventually joining a creative writing class. Then I bought a computer so that I could record my work and print it, which opened up a whole new world for me. My leisure hours are now filled and I have made many new friends and have social contact. *Liza of Lambeth* definitely changed my life.

JACQUELINE MERCER'S STORY
You Can't Afford the Luxury of a Negative Thought
by John-Roger and Peter McWilliams

SYNOPSIS

A self-help book outlining the benefits of positive thinking and helping the reader adopt it into their life. It has been proved that negative thinking can damage a person's health and it affects people by dragging them down mentally, emotionally and physically. The cure proposed is to focus on positive thoughts, to spend less time thinking negatively and to enjoy each moment.

MY STORY

It all started on 10 of December 2008. I have Bipolar Disorder, or Manic Depression as most people used to call it, and through my system being overloaded with too many strong drugs I was quickly becoming very ill. My whole body was becoming toxic and I was at risk of all my organs shutting down, so I was admitted to a Psychiatric Hospital where I was put in Ward 18. Big Mistake!!!

I thought this was how my life would be, a sad, lonely, confused, but mostly scared, human being. I had never been in hospital before, so being around other mentally ill people frightened the life out of me. One night after sitting outside in the garden for hours I decided it was too cold, so I started walking around the ward, going down corridors, through swing doors, not really taking anything in, when I came across the sitting room. As I was picking up the books, which included The Bible and *Boyracers* by Alan Bissett, looking half-heartedly I noticed a book called *You Can't Afford The Luxury Of A Negative Thought*. I thought 'How ironic, isn't that why we're in hospital? Because we can't be positive about anything?'

Anyway, I started reading and I realised that all the things in there were things I knew already but wasn't able to use in everyday life as I wasn't ready. As the days rolled by I read a little more but still wasn't in the right place to take any of the advice.

When I was discharged I decided to get a copy of the book. And in my darkest moments I never gave up – one day I would wake up in a better frame of mind. Each day when I thought 'I can't take life anymore' I read a bit of the book and I tried to take a bit of the advice until it actually started sinking in.

The first day I no longer feared living I actually started to feel better.

I now feel better than I have in years and I live with the book. Now when I feel low or unsure I pick up the book, which I keep by my bed, and I know I'll never be lonely or scared again.

EWAN MORRISON'S STORY

Tropic of Cancer

by Henry Miller

SYNOPSIS

A fictional account of Miller's adventures amongst the prostitutes and pimps, the penniless painters and writers of Montparnasse, *Tropic of Cancer* is an extravagant and rhapsodic hymn to a world of unrivalled eroticism and freedom. *Tropic of Cancer*'s 1934 publication in France was hailed by Samuel Beckett as 'a momentous event in the history of modern writing'. The novel was subsequently banned in the UK and the USA and not released for publication for a further 30 years.

MY STORY

The only book in my parents' bookcase which was turned the wrong way round with the spine hidden was *Tropic of Cancer* by Henry Miller. Their idea was, no doubt, one of caring parental censorship: they didn't want the novel that led to the rewriting of US laws on pornography to fall into my 13-year-old hands. Copies had to be illegally smuggled into the US until the 1960s and a publisher did ten years in jail. Given that my parents were liberal leftists and their bookshelf also included texts by Erica Jong, Aldous Huxley, Jean-Paul Sartre and Vance Packard, I realised that the hidden book had to be pretty radical. I stole it and hid it under my bed.

One might worry that I would have been corrupted by the book. Thankfully, at that point I found it totally incoherent; the page-long sentences unwinding like the ramblings of some drunken poet, wandering from meal to meal, drink to drink, from one sexual adventure to the next through the streets of Paris and Brooklyn. The surrealist stream-of-consciousness style, the impossible mixture of social commentary and autobiographical ranting, did not provide me with the tools I required from so-called pornography. The behaviours described were no more extreme than those that happened weekly in my hippy household. I mentally filed it away under 'pretentious modernist experiment'.

It took me 20 years to come back to Miller, and when I found him again, he was a life-saver. Ironically, I found myself living within a mile of his old home in Brooklyn, wandering from drink to drink and bed to bed, dangerously close to total collapse. In many ways, I blamed my downfall on the permissive society that Miller had helped spawn through his influence on the Beats.

Along with medication, a doctor prescribed that I cut out all destructive behaviour and sit quietly each day, taking stock. I needed the company of a book. In a bookshop on Park Slope, Brooklyn, my eyes came to rest on a book, the title of which had worn away. When I picked it from the shelf it fell into three pieces. I bought it for 25 cents. Beneath a cherry tree, I started again to read *Tropic of Cancer*. What came across was not the graphic sex or the experimental prose, but the generous spirit of an author who had made a total mess of his life and somehow from it, created an even bigger mess of a book (that, somehow, saved him).

Rambling, rambunctious, aimless, vain, flawed, with no methodology, a diary of a living catastrophe, it had more heart and vulnerability than any book I have read since. Beneath the cherry blossoms, I started to write a diary as Miller had done, and I learned that even if you have no direction, writing can give you the strength to go on, at least to the next line.

(This story first appeared in *The Independent* on 26 June 2009)

MARGHERITA MULLER'S STORY
The Shadow-Line: A Confessional
by Joseph Conrad

SYNOPSIS

A novel telling the story of a young sailor who captains a ship for the first time and has a horrific voyage where all his crew get sick and he finds out the medicine bottles are full of water. However, he survives the ordeal and 'becomes a man'. A very short bildungs-novelette – almost a short story but with very intense moments, particularly when the protagonist is alone at night on the deck.

MY STORY

In 1998, I started reading some of Conrad's novels again and kept going for a couple of years.

I only remember distinctly *The Shadow-Line*. By the time I finished reading it I wanted to move out of my country sooner rather than later, something I had delayed beyond belief, most of my life.

I needed to get out of a comfort zone that had become anything but comfortable. As I refused to find reassurance in an impermanent well-being (a good job, a nice house), I simply had to leave.

The notion that Conrad had settled in England at the age of 37 somehow drew a connective picture for me, I could visualise this kind of change for myself. It helped me taking the difficult step of leaving Italy for a future, completely unknown life in Glasgow in 2000, a step I have not ever regretted, even in the bleakest moments.

I felt I was crossing that 'shadow-line' that Conrad mentions in the book, a divide between dark and light – a shadow projected by one of the sails on the deck, the young captain crosses that divide – and looks at himself. He becomes a man.

DONALD S. MURRAY'S STORY
Kidnapped
by Robert Louis Stevenson

SYNOPSIS

This is the story of 16-year-old David Balfour, an orphan, who after being kidnapped by his villainous uncle manages to escape and becomes involved in the struggle of the Scottish Highlanders against English rule.

MY STORY

Let's be honest about it, to misquote a certain newspaper a good number of issues ago, it's 'the pictures wot dun it'.

There were a large number in the edition of Robert Louis Stevenson's *Kidnapped* my dad gave me for my ninth birthday. Their artist, Dudley Watkins, was familiar to me from the few pages of the *Sunday Post* I enjoyed reading when it arrived late every Monday evening in our two-storey but and ben in the Hebrides. Normally, he told of the adventures of a large and dysfunctional family, The Broons, and Oor Wullie, a lad who sported an unfortunate hairstyle and style of clothing – dungarees and tackety boots. This time, however, his black-and-white pictures were not designed to illustrate comic scenes. Neither was there a tenement house or steel bucket in sight. Instead, they told the infinitely thrilling story of a chase across the Highlands and involved two characters, Allan Breck Stewart and David Balfour, in the aftermath of the Jacobite rebellion in 1745.

I probably identified more than a little with the tale. In my wilder fantasies, I probably saw myself as being like David Balfour. In the drawings, he was pictured as being young, tall, dark and handsome – something which, if I succeeded in ignoring a great deal of evidence to the contrary, I could easily imagine myself to be. He was also a Lowlander who, after he had been washed ashore in the Highlands, was struggling to understand the natives. As a boy who had just moved 'up north' from East Kilbride, it was a role that I was born to play. I was, after all, struggling with the Gaelic alphabet that lacked such basic letters as 'W, X, Y and Z'.

And then there was the landscape. The old crumbling manse in the village could double as Ebenezer Balfour's House of Shaws. (There were a number of unshaven, miserly old men who might have taken on the part of Ebenezer). The tidal island near the foot of our family croft could have been the one on which David Balfour was stranded, scouring the rocks for the whelks and limpets our shoreline sprouted in great abundance. Most of all, however, there was Dibadale, a stretch of moorland on the outskirts of the village. Close my eyes and it could have contained the place where the central action, the gunning down of Colin Campbell, the man known as the 'Red Fox', took place. There was a slope where an assassin could lie stretched and hidden, rocks where a clansman holding a rifle might be concealed. It was an act which, in my mind, I performed again and again, shooting down any lad with ginger hair who had the misfortune to head my way.

In short, *Kidnapped* taught me that exciting stories did not just happen elsewhere – but anywhere my imagination wanted them to occur, even my home parish of Ness.

RUAN PEAT'S STORY

The Count of Monte Cristo

by Alexandre Dumas

SYNOPSIS

The ultimate 'time solves all problems, and revenge is sweet but not needed' story. The best revenge is to live well.

MY STORY

As a bullied teen I read this novel and realised that I didn't need to get back at my tormentors this week or even next, I realised that I didn't have to get down to their level and I could wait and enjoy my own life. Revenge always has more effect on the one who does it than on the others on whom it is done. Live well and do well is a much more effective reply to those who would bring us down.

ELAINE POMERANSKY'S STORY
The Diary of Anne Frank
by Anne Frank

SYNOPSIS

A personal diary of a Jewish girl living in an attic, whilst hiding from the Nazis in 1940s Holland during the Second World War.

MY STORY

I first read *The Diary of Anne Frank* when I was 13, the same age as the author, Annelies Marie Frank (known as Anne), who'd written it whilst incarcerated in an attic for two long years. Annelies was a normal teenager, highly intelligent, energetic and sociable; experiencing the same emotions and desires of other girls her age. But like me, Annelies was Jewish. As I wept over the entries as a 13-year-old in Essex, I realised that if I'd been in 1940s Holland I too would have lived with the same fear as Anne Frank, in hiding in order to survive the German political regime; a victim of the Gestapo. Yet it is Annelies's ongoing 'normality' that makes the story all the more harrowing. She is honest, naïve, and naked to her reader; exposing every thought and feeling in her adolescent mind.

Having read of her two-year fight for survival, being privy to all her hopes and dreams, I learnt that after the years of suffering and anguish she doesn't make it to freedom and died in Bergen-Belsen concentration camp. It was then I realised that if the British soliders hadn't sacrificed their lives to protect British citizens, then I too would have died in a concentration camp like Anne Frank. This book shows Annelies to be more than a respected author and a noble and courageous girl; her story has managed to touch the very heart and soul of her readers across the globe. She touched my soul at the age of 13. Her work made me realise the nature of humanity and the importance of words. Words that could sway a whole nation towards discrimination and worse. Words that could persuade medics, scientists and politicians to exterminate millions of people as lesser beings. Words that could also be used to bring hope, pleasure, education and inspiration to the reader. Words are all powerful. And despite her own tragic death, Annelies Marie Frank, through her diary, through her words, has become immortal.

LEON A.C. QUALLS'S STORY

Swing Hammer Swing!

by Jeff Torrington

SYNOPSIS

A novel written in Glaswegian dialect following Tam Clay, 1960s Glasgow slum-dweller, father-in-waiting and wordsmith manqué, as he stumbles through the drink-sodden world of the Gorbals underclass on a mini-odyssey of self-discovery.

MY STORY

I was given a copy of *Swing Hammer Swing!* by my tutor, a Liverpudlian, teaching me creative writing on a degree course in Wales. And what was he trying to teach a Glaswegian? How to write appropriately with Glaswegian vernacular. Up until then I thought that my journey as a writer would only allow me to express myself in standardised English. Little did I know that I could write authentic Glaswegian dialogue, mixed in with English narration and a sprinkling of Scottish banter to create a recipe far greater than I could ever imagine; and thus, gone were the insipid characterisations of mad, mental folk of bygone personal memories, to be replaced by something familiar, something tangible, something real. And all thanks to the late Jeff Torrington and his debut novel.

Then, when writing my own Glaswegian fiction I found it extremely difficult to pin down what was an appropriate amount of vernacular to use.

Should it be in standardised English and thus pander to the broadest possible audience?

Should it be fully Glaswegian from character dialogue to narrator? Or can there be a mix which allows the Glaswegian soul to blossom whilst inviting as many readers as possible to join the party? This is where *Swing Hammer Swing!* showed me the way.

Torrington used the mix of standardised English and Glaswegian vernacular dialogue to supreme effect, judging each and every word on its own merits, to be approached and pronounced in the manner that the context and situation of the moment demanded.

Swing Hammer Swing! is a truly magnificent novel, and Torrington's use of language is phenomenal. Non-native readers may find the plashing of Glaswegian vernacular a bit tricky, but if you can keep with it, it is certainly a worthwhile journey: funny, tragic and ultimately a classic.

It really has changed my life. Without it, I may have given up on my writing.

Without it I wouldn't have fallen in love once more with my literary kin.

And if nothing else, Torrington's sheer determination to finish the novel has inspired me like no other. It took him 30 years to complete, and when asked by a journalist why it had taken so long, he inimitably replied, 'Ah couldnae find ma pencil' – a show of great humour echoing the very nature of the characters he had written, and playing down the importance of how hard he had worked on refining the text.

A great book and a great man. If my tutor had not given me this book, my life would surely have been all the poorer for it.

ELAINE RENTON'S STORY
The Forest is My Kingdom
by Janet Carruthers

SYNOPSIS

Written in 1952, this illustrated book tells about Bari, an orphan, who is brought up in Northern Ontario. His love of animals and nature is only matched by his love of drawing these animals. He befriends an Indian boy with special needs and the story chronicles their adventures together.

MY STORY

Bari Bradbrooke loved spring, and so did an eight-year-old girl from Bainsford. My granddad had worked in Carron Ironworks since he was a boy and, thanks to his labours in Dante's *Inferno*, we owned a holiday house.

Now, don't think of a whitewashed, craw-stepped gable sort of holiday house. Forget about turreted country piles with fishing rights on rushing rivers. No, imagine more of a big garden shed in the middle of nowhere. Think of a dry toilet with a clanking bucket, emptied daily by Granddad. Only the sheep saw his dignified procession, early each morning, across to the midden.

For weeks at a time, I left my pals with their chalky peevers and multi-coloured Chinese skipping ropes. I swapped the Carron, a swollen, slimy slug of a river, silvered with pollution, for a verdant space where Gran and I got water from a tumbling burn.

We called our holiday house The Hut and I spent every spare moment there with my grandparents and boxes of books. Even better, I was allowed to read these books without any type of censoring. How did you think an eight-year-old girl from Bainsford knew about Dante's *Inferno*?

The Hut was furnished with cast-offs, and toffs must be careless, because we had a Clarice Cliff bowl for our fruit and Sylvac planters for the busy Lizzies and geraniums. There was always, always another box of second-hand books to be delved into. All the classics, battered by time, thin dusty Reader's Digests, hundreds of them, crammed full of true life stories.

I stole coal, *Railway Children* style, complete with pram, from along the railway line. I worried about growing a hump like someone in *The Pilgrim's Progress*. I looked for mad ladies locked in attics on my *Jane Eyre* days. I searched for Ginger, Black Beauty's pal, to save him from the knackers' cart.

Then one rainy day I found a duck egg blue book at the bottom of a mildewed box. The dust-jacket was missing, but some precise green print informed me that it was an Oxford Children's Library book. I opened it and stepped inside. My imagination ran riot, while I ran wild with my new friend, Bari.

I lost *The Forest is My Kingdom* over 40 years ago. Thanks to this competition and the internet, I sourced a copy and reading it again has delighted me.

How much influence did this book have? I live in a rural location, surrounded by animals. My oldest friend was Canadian and I'm a special needs teacher, with a flair for little black and white drawings.

Bari's wicked stepfather said to him, 'There's to be no more of this 'ere scribblin' an' drawin''.

Well, I don't think so!

MARK RICE'S STORY
The Hitchhiker's Guide to the Galaxy
by Douglas Adams

SYNOPSIS

The first book in the series of the same name, following Arthur Dent who is catapulted from his mundane life into events on a universal scale, beginning with alien invasion and the destruction of the earth. Told with humour, absurd logic and an eccentric British voice which observes the surreal nature of everyday life.

MY STORY

As a child, I frequently sneaked out of bed at night to sit in the back garden and gaze at the stars in wonder. Though barely out of nappies, I was hungry for answers to the deepest existential questions. I didn't yet realise that, in order to make sense of the answers, I first had to understand the questions. This knowledge came to me one dreich day in 1982 while my Dad and I sheltered from the rain in an East Kilbride bookshop. One book grabbed my attention more than all the others: amid the psychedelic colours on its cover were the words *The Hitchhiker's Guide to the Galaxy*. The back of the book's jacket proclaimed 'Don't Panic' in large, bold letters, so I didn't panic. Instead, I asked my father if he would buy me the book. That serendipitous event introduced me to the wonderful humour and inventiveness of Douglas Adams.

I've read the book multiple times. My enjoyment doesn't diminish with each read; quite the opposite. When, as a ten-year-old, I read it for the first time, I had an epiphany: writing could be both side-splittingly funny and jaw-droppingly creative. *The Hitchhiker's Guide to the Galaxy* showed, in a way I've never seen bettered, that literary genius and mastery of humour need not be mutually exclusive. It made me want to write, not in the cold factual way I'd been taught to write, but by setting my mind free to create its own universes. Douglas Adams taught me that a beautiful juxtaposition is born when stories of human (and alien) silliness are recounted against a backdrop of cosmically relevant events. Perhaps that's the thing I like most about Adams' writing: it celebrates the preposterous, doing so without apology and on a breathtaking scale. He had an amazing ability to point out the absurdity of human behaviour, but to do so with humour rather than nastiness. The light-hearted sense of wonder which permeates every page resonated so strongly within me that it filtered into both my life and my writing.

His writing has that effect on me: it inspires; it makes the Universe seem funny but scarily vast, simultaneously silly and significant; it broadens horizons to a staggering degree; it raises the bar for undiluted creativity. *The Hitchhiker's Guide to the Galaxy* is cleverness and creativity run amok. Adams' description of the way in which the Vogon spaceships hang in the sky when they arrive to destroy Earth showcases his unquestionable genius.

Douglas Adams died in 2001, but his legacy lives on. His writing continues to amaze and amuse me. Thank you, Douglas Adams.

CAROLYN ROBERTS'S STORY
Longmans English Larousse
by Owen Watson

SYNOPSIS

A reference dictionary which comprehensively encompasses the English language.

MY STORY

When I say that *Longmans English Larousse* changed my life, I don't mean the publication in general. I mean one specific copy, and I can tell you exactly where it is right now. It's about 45 miles away, sitting on my dad's bookcase, in the right-hand corner, above the cupboard and diagonally beneath the front-opening bar. It's been there all my life, nestling between *Pears Encyclopaedia* and several books about World War I.

This short fat book was an anchor in our lives. We were – are – a wordy family, not to mention an inquisitive and argumentative family, and the Larousse was our source of both knowledge and peace. It was consulted in every debate about a word's meaning, every spelling query and every bitter Scrabble dispute. In those pre-internet days, we accepted the wisdom of the Larousse as utterly as if it had been chiselled into tablets of stone before our very eyes, and would subside, satisfied that order had been wrought from chaos, meaning from absurdity, and that undoubtedly all was right with the world.

It was not, visually, an attractive book. Its thin cover had some-how survived decades of being yanked from the shelves and waved triumphantly by whoever had turned out to be correct on that occasion. The torn, light brown paper with its pictures of solemn books piled one upon the other and its bulky white typography betrayed its 1960s origins. Even its name was ugly. To this day, I have no idea what a Larousse is, and I am somehow reluctant to look it up, as if to do so would destroy some enduring childhood myth.

The Larousse taught me many things besides simple definitions. It taught me to prize knowledge over ignorance, to value taking the time to find out the facts over muddling along with approximations. It taught me how lucky I was to be brought up in a household with a respect bordering on reverence for language and the written word. It taught me how to throw down some spectacular triple word scores in Scrabble.

It's out of date and little-used now, but I still like to take the Larousse out when I go home, to inhale its familiar smell and turn its fragile pages. It may not be as fast or as current as Wikipedia, but to me, it will always have meaning.

PAULINE RODGER'S STORY

Across the Barricades

by Joan Lingard

SYNOPSIS

This novel is about two adolescents, Kevin and Sadie, from opposite sides of the cultural divide in Belfast during the Troubles, who fall in love and encounter prejudice and hatred from those around them.

MY STORY

I was 14 years old when I first read this book. My preferred reading material at the time was, dare I admit it, my nana's Mills and Boon novels, which she'd sneak to me when she came to visit. I thought this book was a love story too – a boy meets girl, they fall in love, circumstances are difficult but love conquers all, kind of book.

I got more than I bargained for.

Despite the 'happy' ending, I recall being left shocked by the brutality and ruthlessness of the religious bigotry. Whilst reading the book, I was also confused by some of the terminology and constantly had to stop to find out meanings of words I had probably heard before but had never thought to understand. Words like 'Mick,' 'Proddie,' 'Fenian,' 'IRA,' 'Provos,' and the significance of King Billy and the years 1690 and 1916.

The book opened my eyes and highlighted my lack of knowledge. Prior to reading the book, I recall mentions in news reports of car bombs, soldiers being killed at road blocks and pub bombings, but beyond that I had no idea of the history behind or the devastating consequences of the 'Troubles'.

The setting of the book, with its vivid description of the risks of day to day life on the streets of Belfast, made me compare my own upbringing with that of Kevin and Sadie's. This comparison was made even the more poignant by the fact that I was a Catholic girl, attending a predominately Protestant school, with a Catholic mother and Protestant father. I had not experienced the bigotry or the prejudice but having read this book I was forced to confront the threat and danger my family would have faced, had we been living in another part of Britain.

My teenage love story had turned out to be so much more than expected.

MICHAEL ROSEN'S STORY
Great Expectations
by Charles Dickens

SYNOPSIS

A novel which incorporates a mystery and a morality tale, it tells
the story of Pip, a poor village lad, and his expectations of wealth.
The cast of characters includes kindly Joe Gargery, the loyal convict
Abel Magwitch and the haunting Miss Havisham.

MY STORY

My father read this to us in a tent near the North Yorkshire Moors
when I was 13. I can remember it being a moment where I first had
a sense that a novel is often about someone's passage through society
and that this isn't easy or uncomplicated. My father was brilliant
at voices – especially London ones. One moment he could do
Magwitch as a rough, threatening character, the next the forlorn and
posh Miss Havisham, the haughty Estelle and so on. His favourite
was Jaggers though, with his peremptory dealings with Pip. I
remember wishing that I could not only be someone who could act
and read and do voices like my father, but also be someone who
could write as brilliantly as Dickens. This is a book that brilliantly
expresses the way in which we all alter our views of ourselves as we
get older. The book has an older Pip looking at how a younger Pip
behaved and thought, so we are constantly to-ing and fro-ing
between a young Pip and an old Pip. There's no sentimentality in
this. At times the older Pip is rueful, others embarrassed. And just
as there is with our own memories, there's something helpless about
it: you can't change the past. You did those stupid, crass things.

Eventually the young Pip 'catches up' with the old Pip and this
is a moment where we might hope for wisdom, or happiness or
resolution. Dickens wrote two endings for the book, and I much
prefer the unresolved one. The neat and tidy resolved version makes
Pip appear too 'right', too 'correct' in the outcome of his journey
and development. I think it's much more human (and humane) to
have him unable to control his circumstances in the way that he
would most like.

JANE ROWLANDS'S STORY
Little Women
by Louisa May Alcott

SYNOPSIS

The novel follows the lives of four sisters—Meg, Jo, Beth and Amy March. It is loosely based on the author's childhood experiences.

MY STORY

When I was eight years old, along with my four younger siblings I was dramatically whisked off by professionals into the darkest night. Thankfully taken into care, our parents were at long last deemed unfit. You can imagine how traumatic that was for us, because despite having the parents from hell... that hell was all we ever knew.

My first year in care was amazing, I felt like I had been taken to live on a different planet... I was learning new routines, new social skills and along with my already overly-keen observational skills, I felt almost like an alien. In my hellish family, we had never celebrated Christmas before, so you can imagine my excitement when learning I was going to be getting a sack at the end of my bed packed with goodies.

That first Christmas I could hardly sleep... On waking that morning, I was completely overwhelmed that anybody would want to give me fine-looking toys and books, so when the exhilaration waned and I calmed to look at all the items individually, I found myself mesmerised with a beautiful book called *Little Women*. I sat cross-legged on my little bed and began to read the delightful print. I stopped occasionally and stroked the book because I had never, ever owned anything so beautiful in all my life. When called for breakfast with the other children I didn't move, I wanted to breathe in, digest and then read the book some more. The reason this book affected me so dramatically was within the pages of Louisa's experiences with her family, it showed me quite clearly that there was hope for me and I would be loved, wanted and taken care of by my new family.

I was the eldest child in my family; I had always been the bearer of my parent's wrath... so being the eldest I always wanted someone to take care and protect me. Whilst reading *Little Women* I very often dreamed about the character Jo March; I would dream she was my eldest sister and she took good care of me, showing me what life and its adventures were all about, she always made me feel safe and secure.

I'm no longer that little eight year old... but my love for that book and its sequels never ended, I was sure to bring my own daughter up on the beautifully written saga of the *Little Women*.

ESTHER PHOEBE RUTTER'S STORY
Sunbathing in the Rain
by Gwyneth Lewis

SYNOPSIS

A biography meets self-help book which draws on literature and poetry. Written in response to her own experiences of depression, the Welsh National Poet addresses the history of depression in this creative, liberating, and cheerful book.

MY STORY

After experiencing a severe nervous breakdown at the age of 22, I had no idea how to piece my own life back together. Nothing seemed to make much sense: my education seemed a burden that I was desperate to escape from, all my ambition had evaporated overnight, I felt unable to laugh or even be in the same room as people I had once considered my closest friends. All the literature I had read about depression and mental illness seemed to focus on medication, self-control, and vague references to 'talking therapies'. Terrified of my own thoughts and even more mistrustful of those around me, the only thing which offered comfort, understanding, and the possibility feeling alive again was *Sunbathing in the Rain*. My mother bought it for me after hearing it broadcast on Radio 4 and recognised the symptoms Lewis described as being very similar to what I seemed to be going through. I clung to it as a slender and dependable thread of sanity, rereading it every time I felt unsure of myself and my decisions. It is brilliantly – if bleakly – funny, practical, and readable. In the two years since I became ill, I can honestly say that this book not only saved my life, but allowed me to love living again.

JANE RYAN'S STORY
Asterix in Switzerland
by René Goscinny and Albert Uderzo

SYNOPSIS

Gaul was divided into three parts. No, four parts – for one small village of indomitable Gauls still held out against the Roman invaders. Quaestor Sinusitus turns up in Gaul to investigate the creative accountancy of Governor Varius Flavus. When the quaestor is poisoned, he turns to Getafix the druid and the other Gauls for help.

MY STORY

The first I knew of Asterix books was when I spotted them horizontally stacked at the end of a dusty old shelf in a dusty old house on Mull. They were holding up a set of damp-inflated Alistair McLeans and Desmond Bagleys and I'd flicked dully through the Reader's Digest Book of Out of Focus Wildflowers before opening *Asterix in Switzerland*.

At nine I was emotionally outgrowing Enid Blyton so this book came at the right time and was probably responsible for propelling me from the early reader stage to the world of grown-ups. There were delicious innuendos that would take me years to figure out and hieroglyphic writing that had me questioning everything from the meaning of an orgy to the translations of Latin sayings. Sometimes I had to turn the book upside down to see if the names made better sense that way.

Asterix in Switzerland gave the main characters, Asterix and Obelix, the opportunity to go on a mission of life-saving importance. It also provided the writer, Goscinny, and the illustrator, Uderzo, with the means to have a gentle laugh at Switzerland's expense (as they did with every country involved in their titles). The story matches up the Swiss idiosyncrasies of cuckoo clocks, Swiss cheese and dodgy bank accounts with the malpractices of the Roman Empire – to hilarious effect.

Of course, it's not the story alone that makes it compulsive reading. The illustrations are wonderful, sharp line drawings that pay attention to the smallest historical details. I couldn't take my eyes off the colours or the expressions on the faces of the many characters. There was so much to look at and so much to read. I never thought of these stories as comics. For me they were comedy, absolutely, but more they were a powerful magnet into an industry of paint and pen and words that I have never tired of.

A full fortnight of summer rain not only made me an Asterix fan but also someone who has never stopped reading, drawing or writing since I first set eyes on them. Almost 40 years later I am still besotted by these clever books.

SAÏD SAYRAFIEZADEH'S STORY

Krapp's Last Tape

by Samuel Beckett

SYNOPSIS

A short play – a solo piece where the character of Krapp, an old man, listens to a tape of himself 30 years earlier.

MY STORY

The first time I encountered *Krapp's Last Tape* I was bored. The occasion was an initial read-through in a small Pittsburgh, Pennsylvania theatre that was producing an evening of five short Beckett plays, one of which I had been cast in.

I was 23 years old at the time and had a grand opinion of my acting ability as well as what the future held for me. Meanwhile, I was enduring a dreary existence, chronically single, jobless, antisocial – with the exception of theatre – and living alone on the outskirts of the city. I was convinced that things were about to change and that all I had to do was wait. There was a nagging awareness, though, that if there was any hope of altering my life, artistically and emotionally, I had to take it upon myself and move to New York. I had been contemplating this for several years but I was paralysed by the prospect of leaving a city I had lived in most of my life and that was so comforting. So instead I decided to just wait.

It was a cold night in January 1992 when I, along with several actors, sat around a folding table and read from the five Beckett plays that comprised the evening. I had been cast in *Rough for Theatre One* where I played an energetic and conniving invalid. I liked my play. And I liked all of the other plays excluding *Krapp's Last Tape*, which struck me as a convoluted and pointless story, about an old man named Krapp who listens to a tape recording he made of himself 30 years earlier.

Four weeks of rehearsals passed. It was now February. I was still single. And still waiting. The night before we opened I was afforded my only chance to sit in the audience and watch the other plays of the evening. I found them all quite entertaining, charged as they were with Beckett's darkly humorous vision of life. The final play was *Krapp's Last Tape* and it began with the actor, made up to look elderly, sitting at a desk with a tape recorder and a lone light bulb dangling above him. This was proceeded by ten wordless minutes of eating bananas that were absolutely hilarious. I laughed aloud in the empty theatre. And after that the story proper began with Krapp listening to the tape recording of his younger self.

Suddenly it was no longer funny.

The juxtaposition of watching a solitary old man in his dark apartment was unsettling. Furthermore, it was evident that the young man in the recording had an inflated view of himself and his possibilities while we, the audience, were given to understand that what had resulted 30 years later were missed opportunities, lost love, and abject isolation. Beckett's message was simple: time passes.

Sitting in the audience I thought about how I was only 23 years old, but that one day, sooner than I expected, I would be 33 years old, and then I would be 43, and that it was possible that I would end up, in my old age, exactly the person I was now, still dreaming of change.

'Perhaps my best years are gone,' the young Krapp says at the close of the play, his pompous tone slightly diminished. 'When there was a chance at happiness.'

And with the tape recorder running on in silence, the old Krapp stares out at the audience, a look of defeat, as I stared back in horror.

I might not have been so affected by the play if not for the fact that for the next three weeks, three nights each week, I sat in the dressing room having to listen to it until every word had been memorised. And when it was ending I would take my place offstage for the curtain call watching that last moment with Krapp looking out at the audience and the disembodied voice intoning, 'Perhaps my best years are gone. When there was a chance of happiness.'

The following year I was living in New York City.

ALEX SHEPHERD'S STORY

War Picture Library

by Various Authors

SYNOPSIS

A children's comic book series published in the late 1950s – early 1960s. The stories were composed of black-and-white drawings and were fictional tales of derring-do from the Second World War.

MY STORY

When I was a boy my life was changed regularly on the first Monday of every month. I can still recall the thrill felt as the four latest editions of the comic book *War Picture Library*, bound together in comradeship by a thick, brown, rubber band, were launched like paratroops through my letter box.

Their short descent was followed by a surprisingly muted landing on the hallway floor, as if echoing the sound of an unexploded shell fired from the pages of one of that month's stories. As a baby boomer, born three years after the Second World War, from an early age I was fascinated by that recently ended conflict. Facts and images seeped into my young imagination as easily as mustard gas into the lungs of front line soldiers from an earlier war to end all wars. My childhood was partly shaped by the effects of the war, as was that of the rest of my family and society in general. Being still too young to fully appreciate adult history books, *War Picture Library* filled the gap until my reading skills and intellect were sufficiently developed to tackle such learned works. No doubt, on reflection, the characters in the comics were stereotypes, the dialogue stilted and the stories predictable, but at the time they were just wonderful. My interest in the war has both continued and broadened into my '60s. I still like nothing more than to curl up with the latest offering from eminent historians such as Ian Kershaw, Antony Beevor and Michael Burleigh. But I'll always be grateful for the joy that the *War Picture Library* comics gave me and, if the truth be told, I still rather miss the anticipation and thrill of that long ago first Monday of every month.

SARA SHERIDAN'S STORY

Water Music

by T.C. Boyle

SYNOPSIS

Set in 1795, *Water Music* is the rambunctious account of two men's wild adventures through the gutters of London and the Scottish Highlands to their unlikely meeting in darkest Africa.

MY STORY

Water Music changed my life. I'm always banging on about this book. I've bought it as a present for so many people that they are surprised in my local bookshop if it's not in the pile when I get to the till. T.C. Boyle definitely owes me a drink – I've told so many people about his gem of a story of Mungo Park's doomed trips to find the source of the Niger on the cusp of the 18th and 19th centuries.

Water Music is not a story for the faint-hearted, but from the moment I picked it up I was gripped. I'd always loved reading non-fiction history books. There is something fascinating about seeing where different elements of our culture come from, be it the political changes instigated by William Pitt, the economic ideas of Adam Smith or the grim details of the underbelly of life in Edinburgh (where I live) in the social documents that give descriptions of prostitutes living around the Cowgate 200 years ago (how much, I wonder, in that regard, has really changed?). I love language too, of course, and echoing across the ages there is sometimes a hint of where a word started out and a story that forms about how its usage developed – all that stuff fascinates me. I spend a good deal of my time in the library to this day, looking at original material from the archives and that's what I'm really looking for – details that resonate. But until the day I picked up *Water Music* the historical fiction I'd read was a romantic representation of how the world used to be – a series of interesting, fun stories. With this book (kind of like a time machine) it felt as if I was actually there – in the stink of London in 1795 or the squalid, fetid swamps of the Fever Coast in 1806. The story is so well written that it feels natural to imagine what is now an alien era before modern medicine, before the whole world was mapped and package holidayed – a time when, if you had an education and a spirit of adventure, you had the whole of the burgeoning British Empire to explore. And it was dangerous. That kind of adventure isn't available any more and it really grabbed me by the throat.

I probably wouldn't have started writing historical fiction if Boyle hadn't shown me how powerful it could be so maybe, in fact, I owe him a drink after all. His story is in terrible taste, it's filthy, rambunctious and wildly politically incorrect (I do feel I have to warn you) but, like Frankenstein's monster, it lives, and that is a valuable and very rare thing on our bookshelves. He's an absolute master. You should give it a go.

J. DAVID SIMONS'S STORY

Ulysses

by James Joyce

SYNOPSIS

One day in Dublin – 16 June 1904 – in the lives of Stephen Dedalus, Leopold Bloom and his wife, Molly.

MY STORY

Ulysses could be seen as an easy choice for a life-changing novel as it is often cited as the greatest novel of all time – even by those who haven't read it. It took me 20 years to read – I started in my '20s, couldn't finish it, tried again in my '30s and failed. Only in my '40s, did I have the patience, determination and life experiences to complete it. In the same way as opera highlights what can be done with the voice if it were trained to perfection, so Joyce does with the novel. *Ulysses* is the ultimate of what can be achieved in literature – it is what we should all aspire to, even if we can never actually get there. And despite the fact that it is for the most part quite inaccessible – a feature of any writing which normally I abhor – it still manages to seduce me. It is so rich in content, it stretches the mind, it is playful with language, it is vulgar and intellectual at the same time. Its themes are classic and everyday. The rhythm of the language can be quite breathtaking. 'Stately plump Buck Mulligan' – just feel the rhythm and the beat of that first sentence, the plosive sounds 'p' and 'b' – and that's just the first four words. No wonder it changed my life!

CAMERON SINCLAIR'S STORY
101 Essential Golf Tips
by Peter Ballingall

SYNOPSIS

A factual guide to the game of golf. From selecting the right clubs to perfecting your putting technique, this book contains helpful hints to help you improve your golf skills.

MY STORY

101 Essential Golf Tips changed my life by showing me some good tips like the certain amount of clubs/balls/tees that I should put in my golf bag. It also showed me all of the different grips that the professionals use. It showed me all of the different types of swings that I could use for all the different clubs. I learned how to handle the wind and how to get the ball out of the bunker.

After reading this book I have learned all of my strengths and all of my weaknesses out on the course. It is probably my favourite book that I still have because I still take a look at it when I need golf tips and because it helps me improve my game when I go to Aspire Golf Course and Nigg Bay Golf Course. While I was reading *101 Essential Golf Tips* I learned great tips about hitting the ball and then days after I scored my first and second hole-in-one's. I got this book on 21 October 2007 for my tenth birthday; that was also the day I got my first set of junior golf clubs. I read *101 Essential Golf Tips* on the first day I got it and golf is still my favourite sport and hobby.

ANDY STANTON'S STORY
The Wasp Factory
by Iain Banks

SYNOPSIS

The Wasp Factory is a gothic horror novel telling the darkly twisted story of Frank, a profoundly disturbed teenager whose principle sources of entertainment are torturing animals and bumping off unwanted cousins.

MY STORY

One day, when I was a confused young 13-year-old (as opposed to the confused young 35-year-old I am today) I was travelling to school on the Tube when I noticed a man sitting opposite me. He was reading an interesting-looking book. The cover was stark – mostly black – and the title set my imagination racing: *The Wasp Factory*. It sounded cool and harsh and weird and I resolved to read it ASAP.

Later that day – that same day, mind – our English teacher came into the classroom with a stack of books which were not on the syllabus but which he said we should read to broaden our own horizons. Reading, he said, was not something to be confined to academic study. It wasn't a duty but a pleasure. Then he laid his selection of books out on the table. Amongst them was *The Wasp Factory*. It seemed like a sign so I made a beeline for it (sorry, sorry, terrible pun).

And it was everything I was hoping for; ultra-twisted, darkly funny, disturbing, sick and liberating. I was already a big reader but *The Wasp Factory* opened me up to a whole new way of thinking. I felt like I'd found a new friend. A dangerous, unpredictable friend, yes. But sometimes we need to be challenged and shocked out of our normal belief systems.

The Wasp Factory was an essential part of my teenage years and helped me to rethink everything I thought I knew about books. Thank you Iain Banks. Thank you, English teacher. Thank you man sitting opposite me on the tube. You all conspired to help me become the strange individual I am today and I wouldn't have it any other way.

MARGHERITA STILL'S STORY
Green Eggs and Ham
by Dr Seuss

SYNOPSIS

This timeless Dr Seuss classic picture book was first published in 1960, and has been delighting readers ever since. Sam-I-Am is persistently trying to convince the nameless character that green eggs and ham are a delicacy to be savoured.

MY STORY

Green Eggs and Ham by Dr Seuss changed my life when I was seven years old. Firstly I want to make it clear that I had a great childhood, growing up in the '70s on a Scottish council scheme was great for me. I played outside with the rest of the kids on my street, I was never lonely, but my family were poor, properly poor. I didn't know that then so it wasn't important, but now I know that it was one of the factors in my incredibly slow start at school. We never had many books and we certainly didn't have any children's books at home because we couldn't afford them.

My mum was Italian and my dad fought in the Second World War so my home life was interesting but not very good for language development. My speech was mixed with Italian pronunciation, west coast slang and occasional swear words. I have a very strong memory of the infant teachers being horrified at me when I started school, especially the infant mistress who constantly corrected me and took it upon herself to reinforce the fact that I was stupid.

After a year of school I couldn't read and had a real problem telling the difference between blue and purple. Slowly I began to form the idea that I was stupid, and it stuck. For the next two years of school I didn't try too hard and was happy to be left alone, colouring in or counting, which I could do although unnoticed by the infant mistress. My class teachers were frustrated by my lack of progress but I never believed them when they said I could do better.

Then our local library burned down. At the time I had borrowed *Green Eggs and Ham* and despite the requests for borrowed books to be returned I kept it. This became the first book I owned and I loved it. I looked at it again and again until eventually I could read it, cover to cover.

Suddenly I had achieved something that I believed I couldn't and it changed my way of thinking. I wasn't stupid anymore, I started to learn. I learned so fast that I went from the bottom of the class to the top, I went from *Green Eggs and Ham* to a whole feast of books, anything I could get my hands on.

And the rest, as they say, is history. I made my English teacher proud with an A at Higher, one of very few at my school, then achieved what I needed to get where I wanted and now have three kids who have a mountain of books.

Today I teach, and I never tell children they can't, they just can't yet.

GAEL STUART'S STORY
We Learned to Ski
by Sunday Times

SYNOPSIS

An easy-to-read manual about skiing.

MY STORY

In the early 1980s *The Times* published *We Learned to Ski.*

Since childhood I have absolutely loved ice skating, although not the beautiful arabesques and triple sulkos of the figure skating set. No, for me it was speed skating – graceful, fast and powerful.

Skiing I felt must be akin to ice skating, but then I was in my late '20s and I had never made the transition from ice and blade to mountain and ski boot.

The book drew me to it as soon as I noticed the bright yellow snow suit emblazoned on the front cover. The skier was laughing happily, but she was not paralleling confidently down a grand slalom slope. The laughter was in response to her fall!

Along the top margin was a wavy line with little skiers adopting the correct body posture as they easily made their way from the left hand side of the cover to the right, up and down every trough and peak of the wave.

I had never seen anything like it before. A manual that was so beautifully written in such a simple way that, should the reader be found in conversation about skiing, she could be thought of as a seasoned pro!

The next step was to take lessons. I had to learn how to use my edges in a different way, shift my weight and, of course, hills are not level. *We Learned To Ski* was like taking my instructor home with me. Every aspect of my learning was anticipated in my manual and this made my journey from non-skier to skier fast and confident.

I am so grateful to *We Learned to Ski* for introducing me to the sport, for had I not happened upon that book I may never have experienced the joys of skiing... oh and numerous falls!

MARSALI TAYLOR'S STORY

A Guid Cause

by Leah Leneman

SYNOPSIS

A thoroughly researched account of the suffrage movement in Scotland, this book follows the history of women's struggle for the right to vote from the first societies in 1870s Edinburgh and Glasgow, through the Victorian petitions and processions and Edwardian terrorists, to the First World War and Dr Inglis' units on the Russian Front.

MY STORY

I knew almost nothing about the suffrage cause when I began reading; I was more interested in Dr Elsie Inglis' Russian Unit, and knew she'd been suffrage-funded. The vague ideas I had focused on London: women chaining themselves to railings, storming Downing Street and being force-fed. Nobody had ever said anything about Scotland, or explained that Asquith and Churchill's seats here made it a front-line. Nobody had mentioned defiant middle-aged women bombing railway stations and firing houses, or shipping-heiress Janie Allan firing blanks at the police from a revolver. I looked up the Shetland Society, my local, and found a committee here, in 1872.

I read the original Hansard speeches, and longed to kick the pompous MPs who kept saying 'Women don't really want the vote' when thousands of women were petitioning and marching to say that they did. I learned that women wanted the vote to be able to change their lives: to get equal wages, to be allowed to keep their own earnings, to be able to leave violent husbands, to be allowed to go to university. I fulminated over 1912 letters in the local newspaper, with men called 'Patriarch' and 'Observer' saying suffragists couldn't be Christians, and a 'fatherly tap' was good for a woman. And I learned what women really did in the war. They drove ambulances up to the front line, under appalling conditions, over and over again, and nursed the wrecks of men brought back. They serviced planes, ploughed fields, filled shells with gunpowder. One in the Serbian army even commanded a platoon.

Reading this book didn't just change my life; it had a fair effect on others around me. I hassled the local council to place a plaque on the house where the Shetland committee met; I've persuaded the local museum to celebrate their centenary with an exhibition. I joined the Gude Cause March in Edinburgh, in October, with a Shetland banner painted by my sister, and I've spent so much time in the local archives that my husband has begun saying plaintively 'Will this book of yours ever be finished?' Well, it will be, so that Shetland girls can know what their amazing grandmothers and great-grandmothers did to get them the vote. It's a story that shouldn't be forgotten by any of us.

PETER URPETH'S STORY
Hunger
by Knut Hamsun

SYNOPSIS

Hunger is an intense novel about a starving writer, which has attracted readers since its publication in 1890. It's author, Norwegian novelist, dramatist and poet Knut Hamsun won the Nobel Prize for Literature in 1920.

MY STORY

At the age of 16 I found myself commuting to a shipping insurance office in the City of London to toil as a junior in accounts. I had just left school with virtually no qualifications and was very disillusioned, having hated the experience of schooling. But I knew I wanted to read. One lunchtime, I came across a bookshop near the Leadenhall Market which had a stand of colourful books all published by a firm called Picador. I liked the cover of a book called *Hunger* by a Norwegian author, Knut Hamsun. The book was also very short, and seemed a good proposition for the daily train rides. Within two days I was staying on the train in the morning reading this gem, and now found myself riding up and down the line between Romford and Liverpool Street, phoning in sick to cover my new found love. This compelling, intense book changed everything for me. I think in my unhappy and dissatisfied mental state at that time I connected quite personally with the inferiority of the main character, his struggles and his ebbing narratives of pleasure and disappointment. Through this book I had suddenly connected with the immense open field of literature and the imagination. Later that year I started an English A-level night class and books have been my life since. I still have that original copy. Its pages have fallen out, the cover is brittle and brown but it remains a treasure. After *Hunger* I read Hamsun's *Mysteries* and found the joy of rebelliousness both witty and latent with possibilities.

EMMA WALKER'S STORY
Alice's Adventures in Wonderland
by Lewis Carroll

SYNOPSIS

A children's novel about an inquisitive girl, Alice, who one boring summer afternoon, follows a white rabbit down a rabbit-hole. At the bottom, she finds herself in a bizarre world full of strange creatures, and attends a very strange tea party and croquet match. This witty and unique story mixes satire and puzzles, comedy and anxiety, to provide an astute depiction of the experience of childhood.

MY STORY

I first read *Alice's Adventures in Wonderland* when I was seven years old. While I was a ferocious reader, at seven I still needed pictures to accompany my story tales, so when I was handed a book without any pictures inside I wasn't happy. That is, until I started to read. The story of Alice falling down the rabbit hole, running in a caucus race, meeting Cheshire Cats and Mad Hatters while eating cakes and drinking potions which made her grow and shrink was more than enough to stimulate my imagination into overdrive. I was as high as the Caterpillar by the time I finished the novel and wanted more.

Instead of moving onto Alice's next adventure with a looking glass, I picked up a pen and began to write. Unaware of plagiarism at such a young age I rewrote every last word of the unabridged version making just one vital edit – the word 'Alice' was replaced with my name, 'Emma'. With that small but essential rewrite I had become Alice and every adventure I pursued after that was done so with the knowledge that the White Rabbit may just be around the corner.

I now have a framed painting of Alice peering into Wonderland by my front door to remind me that every day is an adventure and nothing is ever quite as it seems.

HEATHER WALLACE'S STORY

Emma

by Jane Austen

SYNOPSIS

Beautiful, clever, rich – and single – Emma Woodhouse is perfectly content with her life and sees no need for either love or marriage, but loves exercising her superior judgement in matchmaking her friends and acquaintances. Emma's plans unravel and she gets much more than she bargained for.

MY STORY

I first attempted to read *Emma* when I was 19 and on holidays with my parents. Two chapters in and I gave up – what an unlikable, arrogant, meddlesome character Emma was, always in charge and imposing her ways. I had no sympathy for her and no wish to spend any more time in her company.

Fast forward a few years, as a 23-year-old I was caring for a recently widowed parent who took refuge in ill health to hide from crippling grief. I was in charge of the household in a role reversal, imposing my ways on my parent and bending them to my will.

One morning I picked up *Emma*, where she had lain forgotten on my bookshelf for so long.

The more I read, the more of myself I saw and the character that I had once disdained had transformed into a deeply misunderstood character, and although she is not without fault, she was always trying her best for those around her.

I finished *Emma* in one sitting, and by the end realised where my path may take me unless I started to exercise a little more compassion and acceptance of those around me.

I still have real sympathy for Emma and enjoy the times I revisit her, I'm not sure though that we'd get on if we met in real life, we'd probably both want to be in charge.

ROSIE WELLS' STORY
Heidi
by Johanna Spyri

SYNOPSIS

A classic children's novel telling the story of Heidi, a small girl who lives with her grandfather in his little wooden house, high up in the mountains of Switzerland. One day Heidi's aunt arrives and takes her to Clara's home in Frankfurt. Heidi likes her new friend, but she doesn't like living in a big house in the city. Together she and Clara learn about friendship, sacrifice and courage.

MY STORY

Janet and John almost ruined my life, but *Heidi* saved me!

Nearly 60 years ago, my father was injured in an accident. He was not expected to survive. I was shipped off to German relatives, while mother waited for the end.

My early memories of my upbringing by my grandparents and widowed aunt are filled with rhythm: skipping chants, 'Max und Moritz', folk songs sung under lanterns, tales of youth in the 1890s told by my cigar-puffing Opa... Even now, I can recall the charmingly illustrated music books of my cousin's recorder practice.

Contentment was shattered at four. My visa was running out. My father had emerged from hospital. I was escorted home to England by my tear-streaked grandparents. I began to learn the definition of terms. I learned fast, little realising that those brief summer weeks were my crash course into all things English.

One day, Oma and Opa disappeared, swallowed up, gone. Unhappiness, tears, tantrums. To add to my growing sense of alarm, my mother told me that I must attend school...

Although teachers knew I spoke little English, I remember contorted faces, grimacing words I did not understand. Despairing, I threw an empty milk bottle across the room. 'Handkerchief', I sobbed. A handkerchief appeared. The magic of words!

I buckled under, conformed, collecting words and phrases for survival. 'The farmer's in his den' and other schoolyard chants became familiar, even if I was often the butt of rough handling.

I was literate in German, but that was NOT PERMITTED. So, I became literate in English, reading endless *Janet and John* stories, which threatened to kill any love I had for reading.

Eventually, after many reading misadventures, Johanna Spyri's *Heidi* saved me. The novel, which I read with my mother, spoke about environments and feelings I recognised. I could place myself in Heidi's shoes. Like Heidi, I longed to go home to my family: Opa, Oma, Tante Gilla and Moni. Like Heidi, I was sleepwalking and there were whispered exchanges about my being 'unsettled'. I felt like her long-lost sibling.

I loved the detailed descriptions, the resonant exchanges between characters. Now, I realise that the novel voiced the sort of vivid memories I had heard while cradled on my grandmother's lap. Like Heidi, I began to delight in my growing literacy skills. She gave me optimistic expectations.

My love of reading revived, developed, galloped ahead.

Today, as I sit in my book-lined room, surrounded by Dickens and Hardy, Shakespeare and Chaucer, so many old friends that accompanied me to Scotland, I am grateful for my fractured beginnings as a reader. After all, without the discovery of *Heidi*, what would we have called our daughter?

GILLIAN WHALE'S STORY
The Iron Man
by Ted Hughes

SYNOPSIS

A modern children's anti-war morality tale about a giant iron man, a small boy called Hogarth and a 'Space-Bat-Angel-Dragon' which threatens life on Earth.

MY STORY

'The Iron Man came to the top of the hill. Where he had come from...'

I was a mature student on my first proper teaching practice, in charge of a class of nine-year-olds in a run-down area of Hertfordshire. I felt I was failing. I felt exposed and nervous in front of a full class, especially with the class teacher trying to be inconspicuous and mark books in a corner. It was all much, much harder than I had anticipated. As I was 37 and a mother of three, the college staff thought I ought to find it easy and had allotted me the most difficult placement. I was struggling with class control, with planning for a huge range of abilities, with almost everything. The only thing in my favour was that I still liked the kids, even the many who were constantly giving me grief. I naïvely thought they behaved perfectly for everyone else and so far no one had had the kindness to reassure me otherwise. I was demoralised and not far from giving up.

The afternoon story started as badly as it always had done up to now. I thought I was rubbish at engaging the children's attention. The usual suspects were chatting, poking each other, answering back and generally pretending I wasn't there. I sat it out for a minute or so then just started to read, ignoring the interruptions.

After about half a page I realised that all I could hear was the sound of my own voice reading Ted Hughes' magical, musical words. They were hooked. When I stopped at the end of the first chapter they didn't fidget and chat as I had grown to expect. They wanted more. They asked questions and listened to the answers and to each other. They thought they could try to think what was going to happen next...

I could do it! I didn't give up. I practised hard and got better and had a wonderful career.

MICHAEL WILLIAMS' STORY
Siddhartha
by Hermann Hesse

SYNOPSIS

Hesse's novel follows the journey and education of the Brahmin Siddhartha as he sets out to learn about the ways of the world in an attempt to understand and master his own fear and suffering.

MY STORY

It was 1972, I was 20 years old, had dropped out of University two years earlier, gone to work in the mines in Northern Canada for a winter and was now back in my home town of Hamilton Ontario, working in a factory making sewer pipes. The factory was a mind-numbing, soul-destroying place for me; it was a noisy, dirty, dangerous place where I stood all day pushing and pulling levers, pressurising the pipes with water, looking for cracks and hoping they wouldn't – as they sometimes did – explode. Further down the line from me worked a long-haired fellow who pretty much kept to himself. The older men simply referred to him as 'The Hippie'. I noticed, however, that he read books during his breaks and at lunchtime. One day, he approached me and handed me a dog-eared paperback. 'Here,' he said, 'read this, you look like you could use it. It might save your life.' Then he walked away. 'Thanks!' I shouted after him. He simply raised his hand in acknowledgement, shouting 'Keep it' and went back to work. I looked down at the book in my hand. *Siddhartha* by Hermann Hesse. I had never heard of it or its author. But that night, I began to read. I couldn't put it down. By the time I finished it, I knew what I had to do. Three weeks later, I had quit my job and was headed for the highway, embarking on my own journey to enlightenment. That journey lasted two years as I travelled North America and later, Europe. That journey opened my mind to new ideas, introduced me to strange and wonderful places and people and taught me how to live by my wits. Somewhere along the way, I left that copy of *Siddhartha* in a hostel with a hastily scrawled note on the inside cover instructing whoever found this book to read it and pass it on. More than 30 years later,

I still think of that book and wonder how many hands and minds it might have passed through.

Siddhartha changed the course of my life. It launched me on a journey of self-discovery, which continues to this day. It sent me from that factory and down a road which has seen me become, among other things, a musician, a lover, a social worker, a salesman, an academic, a teacher, a peace activist, an education consultant, a husband, a father, a divorced father and a storyteller. Like Siddhartha, I have learned a great deal about life and love. Unlike Siddhartha, I have not yet fulfilled my destiny... perhaps now is the time to revisit my old dog-eared friend and get reacquainted. Books are like that; they always seem to come along just at the time when you need them most. Thank you Hermann Hesse... and thanks 'Hippie', wherever you may be, for ferrying me across river.

ERIC YEAMAN'S STORY

A School Chemistry for Today

by F.W. Goddard & Kenneth Hutton

SYNOPSIS

A school chemistry textbook used in the 1950s.

MY STORY

In the late '50s, school chemistry was traditional. Oxygen – preparation, properties and uses. Carbon dioxide – preparation, properties and uses. Chlorine – preparation, properties and uses. Hydrogen chloride – preparation, properties and uses. And so on. It was all methodically catalogued in our textbook. And it was all (fairly) conscientiously copied into our jotters.

Then, it was probably early 1959, our teacher gave out a new book – *A School Chemistry for Today* by F.W. Goddard and Kenneth Hutton.

To me, it was like throwing open a door, showing a bright new world of chemicals which I had hardly suspected. I remember taking that book home, and going through it, discovering all sorts of fascinating substances with exciting names. Cobalt. Fluorine. Phosphorus. Manganese. Barium. Even common things, like iron, copper and lead, could have unsuspected chemical reactions.

I spent hours, compiling my own files on these substances, using the book's index to track down each sliver of information, and carefully noting it down.

I don't claim that the book was my sole reason for going on to study chemistry at university, but it undoubtedly inspired me to anticipate the prospect with greater enthusiasm. I went on to teach chemistry, and I can only hope that I managed to convey to my pupils the excitement that I experienced in my explorations of *A School Chemistry for Today*.

SARAH ZAKERI'S STORY

Reading Lolita in Tehran

by Azar Nafisi

SYNOPSIS

In this 'memoir in books', Nafisi, a professor of English Literature, recounts her story of lecturing during the revolution in Iran and of later holding an illicit, all-female book group in her living room, before she left for America.

MY STORY

Growing up in the North East, half Scottish/half Iranian, I have always felt proud to be Scottish. Any glimpse I caught of Iran, through the news or otherwise, told of a terrifying and hostile place where minds were closed, open only to a single ideology, and where women were slaves to their husbands' whims. The thought of it instilled a great, nauseating fear in me. How could women live like this? And then, studying English literature at university, my mind being opened to many ideas, cultures and histories, I felt pity for those, such as women in Iran, who were only exposed to one idea, one rule, one way of living. I couldn't understand how a country, once so rich in culture, could now be so culturally barren.

Then, just after leaving university, while browsing in a bookshop, the incongruous title of this book caught my eye. *Reading Lolita in Tehran* – surely not. But there it was, bringing together two aspects of my life which had seemed entirely separate. The book was a revelation. Not only was there one Iranian woman with a love of English literature, there were lots! And they were just like girls here – gossipy, quick-witted, bitchy, clever, and romantic, with dreams and ambition and a passion for life, love and friendship. I learnt several things – that even in the face of oppression, sexism and fundamentalism, passion can still exist, and, trite though it sounds, that it really doesn't matter what race, colour or nationality you are. Literature is universal and indeed you can feel yourself to be any nationality you like, if you feel an affinity with that culture. Nafisi does a marvellous job of showing how literature is a culture in itself that can reach out to all nations, and she also taught me that being half-Iranian is not something to be frightened by. Nationality and race are things that should be worn proudly but also lightly, for the human spirit will always transcend political divisions.

I also learnt that the combination of coffee, ice-cream and walnuts is worth a try...

Index of Books

101 Essential Golf Tips 120
1984 46, 78
Across the Barricades 106
Alice's Adventures in Wonderland 128
Alone Together 16
Asterix in Switzerland 112
A School Chemistry for Today 136
Black, White and Gold 26
Border Ballads 23
The Boy with the Bronze Axe 59
The Catcher in the Rye 37
A Clockwork Orange 79
Collected Shorter Poems 74
The Count of Monte Cristo 96
Daffodils 54
Dancing on the Edge 38
Danny the Champion of the World 25
The Diary of Anne Frank 97
The Dice Man 36
A Dictionary of the Older Scottish Tongue 68
DK Dinosaur Encyclopaedia 73
The Easy Way to Stop Smoking 60
Emma 129
The End of Mr Y 31
The Fog 28
The Forest is My Kingdom 100
The Golden Treasury 33
Great Expectations 108
Green Eggs and Ham 122
A Guid Cause 125

Heidi 71, 130
The Hitchhiker's Guide to the Galaxy 102
Horrible Histories 66
The Horse's Mouth 85
Hunger 127
The Iron Man 132
It 52
Jane Eyre 18
Kidnapped 94
Krapp's Last Tape 114
Lamb 14
Lassie Come Home 65
Linmill Stories 76
Little Women 109
Liza of Lambeth 87
Longmans English Larousse 104
The Lord of the Rings 80
The Mists of Avalon 69
My Life as a Man 13
Not the End of the World 83
Noughts and Crosses 53
The Once and Future King 39
Portrait of a Young Man Drowning 57
A Portrait of the Artist as a Young Man 35
Piano Course, Book A (The Red Book) 49
Reading Lolita in Tehran 137
The Restaurant at the End of the Universe 62
The Shadow-Line: A Confession 93
Shantaram 44

Siddhartha 134
The Sopranos 63
Southeast Asia on a Shoestring 41
Stuart: A Life Backwards 32
Sunbathing in the Rain 121
Superman: From the '30s to the '70s 48
Swallows and Amazons 55
Swing Hammer Swing! 98
Tiger-Pig at the Circus 82
Tuesdays With Morrie 51

The Unwanted Child 42
Tropic of Cancer 91
Ulysses 119
Walden; or, Life in the Woods 29
War Picture Library 116
The Wasp Factory 121
Water Music 117
We Learned to Ski 124
Weaveworld 20
You Can't Afford the Luxury of a Negative Thought 89

To find out about how you can get involved
in Scottish Book Trust's reading and writing projects
visit **www.scottishbooktrust.com**

Some other books published by **LUATH** PRESS that could change your life

Linmill Stories

Robert McLellan

ISBN 1 906307 23 7 HBK £12.99

The young Rab, under the often-crabbit watch of his granny and his indulgent grandad, goes on adventures as he fishes for *mennans*, handles the responsibility for pumping the kirk organ on the Sabbath and helps his cousins earn pennies for the sweetie shop.

As well as the charming but realistic accounts of his grandparent's farming life, these stories present a captivating relationship between the boy and the natural world in which he experiences the joys and trials of growing up.

It is possible to find light and depth in each of these stories, yet their common engine is neither plot nor character, but McLellan's use of language. It is hard not to agree with J.K. Annand's final assessment that Robert McLellan is 'the greatest writer of Scots prose in the 20th century'.
BOOKS IN SCOTLAND

This must rank [among] the finest prose-poetry of Scottish childhood that we have.
DOUGLAS GIFFORD

Days Like This: a portrait of Scotland through the stories of its people

ISBN 1 906307 97 0 PBK £6.99

We all have days we'll never forget...

Days Like This is a collection of selected stories submitted by people all over Scotland as part of a national project run by Scottish Book Trust and BBC Radio Scotland.

Whether humorous, poignant, dark or surreal, the stories reveal the emotions and dramas at the heart of all human experience – a bald sixteen stone cross-dressing rugby player; a haunted pub basement; a love affair that begins outside a burning disco; a perfect day spent with a toddler – every story is unique, every one a gem.

The book comprises stories from celebrities Irvine Welsh, Roddy Woomble, Siobhan Redmond, Jamie Andrew, Hardeep Singh Kohli and Evelyn Glennie, plus some of their favourite stories.

The Burying Beetle

Ann Kelley

ISBN 1 84282 099 0 PBK £9.99
ISBN 1 905222 08 4 PBK £6.99

The countryside is so much scarier than the city. It's all life or death here.

Meet Gussie. Twelve years old and settling into her new ram-shackle home on a cliff top above St Ives, she has an irrepressible zest for life. She also has a life-threatening heart condition. But it's not in her nature to give up. Perhaps because she knows her time might be short, she values every passing moment, experiencing each day with humour and extraordinary courage.

Gussie's story of inspiration and hope is both heartwarming and heartrending. Once you've met her, you'll not forget her. And you'll never take life for granted again.

Gussie's story is continued in *The Bower Bird*, winner of the 2007 Costa Children's Award, and *Inchworm*.

Gussie fairly fizzles with vitality, radiating fun and enjoyment into everything that comes her way. Her life may be predestined to be short but not short on wonder, glee, the love of things as they really are. It is rare to find such tragic circumstances written about without an ounce of self-pity. Rarer still to have the story of a circum-scribed existence escaping its confines by sheer force of personality, zest for life.
MICHAEL BAYLEY

My Epileptic Lurcher

Des Dillon

ISBN 1 906307 74 1 PBK £7.99

That's when I saw them. The paw prints. Halfway along the ceiling they went. Evidence of a dog that could defy gravity.

The incredible story of Bailey, the dog who walked on the ceiling; and Manny, the guy who got kicked out of Alcoholics Anonymous for swearing.

Manny Riley is newly married, with a puppy and a wee flat by the sea, and the BBC are on the verge of green-lighting one of his projects. Everything sounds perfect. But Manny has always been an anger management casualty, and the idyllic village life is turning out to be more League of Gentlemen than The Good Life. The BBC have decided his script needs totally rewritten, the locals are conducting a campaign against his dog, and the village police-man is on the side of the neds. As his marriage suffers under the strain of his constant rages, a strange connection begins to emerge between Manny's temper and the health of his beloved Lurcher.

Laugh-out-loud funny, this brilliant novel breaks into a convincing Dogspeak that will ring true in any dog-loving household. Complete with all the jealousy and heartbreak that come into any loving relationship, dog-human relations have never been so vividly expressed.

Details of these and other books published by Luath Press can be found at:
www.luath.co.uk

Luath Press Limited
committed to publishing well written books worth reading

LUATH PRESS takes its name from Robert Burns, whose little collie Luath (*Gael.*, swift or nimble) tripped up Jean Armour at a wedding and gave him the chance to speak to the woman who was to be his wife and the abiding love of his life. Burns called one of 'The Twa Dogs' Luath after Cuchullin's hunting dog in Ossian's *Fingal*. Luath Press was established in 1981 in the heart of Burns country, and is now based a few steps up the road from Burns' first lodgings on Edinburgh's Royal Mile.

Luath offers you distinctive writing with a hint of unexpected pleasures.

Most bookshops in the UK, the US, Canada, Australia, New Zealand and parts of Europe either carry our books in stock or can order them for you. To order direct from us, please send a £sterling cheque, postal order, international money order or your credit card details (number, address of cardholder and expiry date) to us at the address below. Please add post and packing as follows: UK – £1.00 per delivery address; overseas surface mail – £2.50 per delivery address; overseas airmail – £3.50 for the first book to each delivery address, plus £1.00 for each additional book by airmail to the same address. If your order is a gift, we will happily enclose your card or message at no extra charge.

Luath Press Limited
543/2 Castlehill
The Royal Mile
Edinburgh EH1 2ND
Scotland
Telephone: 0131 225 4326 (24 hours)
Fax: 0131 225 4324
email: sales@luath.co.uk
Website: www.luath.co.uk